LYDIA'S

GIFT

A novel by Linda Mayo

LYDIA'S GIFT

By Linda Mayo

Copyright 2014 by Linda Mayo

All Rights Reserved

Published by: Linda Mayo
Printed in the United States of America
Copyright © 2014 Linda Mayo
All rights reserved.
ISBN-13:9780615982892
Cover design by Linda Mayo,
Picture by Christi Mayo

DEDICATION

This story is dedicated to my family,

To my brothers and sisters who have stood strong together,

A mother who had a perfect gentle soul,

A father who loved unconditionally,

And, especially, to my daughter who has made me proud every day of her life.

I love you all dearly!

LYDIA'S GIFT

WRITTEN BY: LINDA MAYO

CONTENTS

Special Thanks to those who encouraged my dream

Carolyn Plecker   Kimberly Plecker

Christi Mayo   Brenda Painter

1

COMATOSE

Waking at the usual time, the six a.m. alarm woke me with a jolt. I had been feeling very fatigued, not unlike many mornings before. Getting up was a challenge. I felt I couldn't lift my head off the pillow. When I did, a horrible throbbing was in my head. "Oh no, another migraine!" Sluggishly, I pulled myself up and circled the bottom of my bed. Feeling faint, I stumbled towards the bed, which cushioned my fall as I dropped to the floor. Lying there, a cold sweat poured over me, then blackness.

I had no clue how long I had been unconscious; yet, when I awoke, I became keenly aware of how different I felt. My head no longer throbbed. Still stretched out on the floor, I carefully pulled myself up, clutching the bottom of the bed. I examined myself to make sure nothing was broken from the fall. It was then that I saw it; rather I saw ME, still lying on the floor!

"Am I hallucinating?" I thought. I leaned closer to make sure my imagination hadn't tricked me. It really was me, out cold! "What do I do?" I asked myself, trembling. As I clutched my body, I saw a white glow around the edges of my skin. Panicking, I dashed to my daughter Christi's room to wake her. Thank God she was visiting me for the week.

Bursting into her room she was in solid slumber. As I entered, I screamed, "Christi, wake up, something's wrong!" She didn't move. "Christi," I said much louder, "wake up! What's going on?" Shaking, touching and feeling her, I could see that the skin on her arm didn't move under my touch. Stepping back, stunned, I cried out again. "Oh my! Christi, please wake up. I need your help!" The movie, *Ghost,* suddenly entered my mind. I recalled the leading character Sam, who had to learn the ability to touch or feel by really focusing in on his subject. Leaning closer to Christi's face, and, with my index finger, I rubbed the side of her cheek. She moaned and turned to her side. "It worked!" I did it again, and she positioned herself on her back, slowly waking up. I watched her lazily get up and head towards the door. She was staying in the room directly across from mine, so I was confident she would see me lying at the end of my bed. She strolled by and didn't take the first look toward my room. "Oh my God, Oh my God, Oh my God," I stammered. I was dashing in front of her first this way, then that way, yelling and jumping, but she didn't hear me at all. I was too distraught at this point to calmly focus as before. Christi went into the bathroom and, while she was there, I darted back to my room to look again. Lying there in the same position, I had not stirred. Having studied "out of body" experiences, I found reading about it and living it, are two very different matters. I have always been infatuated with true life stories, of people who had experienced this very thing. I was freaking out trying to rationalize the situation!

Christi came out of the bathroom and headed towards her room. This time she glanced toward my room. "Mom!" she yelled when she saw me. She ran to me and shook me lightly to see if she could rouse me, but I didn't move. She darted to her room, grabbed her cell phone, and called 911. Returning to where I was lying, I heard her tell them as calmly as she could, "please hurry, she's unconscious!" I could hear, even through the phone, the 911 Operator asked, "Is she breathing?"

Christi said, "Yes, but barely."

Leaping up and down in front of her, I shouted, "Good job, Christi, good job!" I ran back and forth in excitement from her room to my room observing the situation. "Put some clothes on before the ambulance arrives," I said, thinking of things to do before the ambulance pulled up outside. I kept forgetting she couldn't hear me. How typical of me to think about appearances at a time like this. I darted back to see what night gown I had on! "Oh good. It's not one of my old dowdy gowns that I don't want to part with, but never want to be caught dead in. Err, funny choice of words! Ok, Ok, what do I do now?" I thought, still in panic mode dashing from room to room. I suddenly recalled how I hadn't been feeling well lately. "Where is this energy coming from now?"

After hanging up with the emergency call, Christi went to her room to change, then, returned to my room. I was happy to see she had replaced her night clothes with a sweat suit.

Christi began dialing my sister Carly, quickly telling her of my predicament. I could hear my sister through the phone saying, "Oh, my God!" We had just lost our mother not that long ago and the pain was still fresh. In the background I could hear sirens approaching, getting closer and closer. Christi was in panic mode by now. Choking back the tears, she told Carly, that she would meet her and my siblings at the hospital.

"She's down the hall in the master bedroom. Follow me," she said as she pointed. The EMT'S went to work on me quickly.

"How is she?" my daughter asked after a few torturous

minutes.

"Her vitals are very weak. We need to transport her to the hospital right away," the rescue attendant said to her in a calm but urgent voice.

"Ok. I'll follow you," she said ready to cry at this point. They placed my lifeless body on the stretcher and rolled me out of the room. As I started to follow, a brilliant beam of light impeded the doorway. The light streamed, resembling sun rays peeking through the dark clouds. Only this light seemed to have small sparkles dispersed inside it. Having observed it, I knew from all of my readings of afterlife experiences that I had to go towards that light.

Moving into the light, I instantly felt I had been lifted. Right away, my body relaxed and peacefulness filled my being. There was no anxiety, nor did I care where I was going. I relaxed and allowed the light to overtake me. I felt trust, love, and warmth from this light.

2

ENTITY

Without realizing how it happened, I suddenly found myself in an upright position. The light that had surrounded me was still swirling. No, I'd say it was *dancing* around me. I watched in awe as this beautiful light took on a life of its own. It was as if the light was taunting me or, perhaps, trying to make me smile. Beholding its brilliance, I noticed a light form taking shape as it came towards me. It too was a light, but it was very different as it took on a person form. Marveling at this new form, the dancing light began moving away from me. If I stopped watching, it seemed to pull away. As you might guess, I was torn between the two. I deeply desired the warmth, love, and peace it provided. If the light left, I feared those feelings may leave too. The first and second light began to merge until; I could no longer distinguish the two forms as they became one.

"Hello, Lydia. It is so good to see you," the Entity announced. The image knew my name as if we had already met and were long-time friends. As he continued speaking with me, his form began taking on a human density, showing his image in male form as an earthly being. The light, so prevalent only moments before, radiated only from the edges of his skin. He was picturesque. His skin glowed with radiance, flawless in every way. I couldn't stop staring at him. I was mesmerized by his features. His eyes sparkled with love, his hands radiated warmth. His smile was like a soothing caress. His voice was a calming breeze. He reached for my hand and I placed mine in his. At his very touch, I immediately became all knowing. I knew who he was. My knees buckled in reverence! This could not be real! I looked around to see if anyone else noticed *who* was standing with me! I could see no one. Just blank space, so my attention went back to him. Holy mother of God (in a good way), it was Jesus himself! Ok. Someone slap me! This is the best dream I have ever had!

He laughed out loud. Oh my gosh, he knew what I was thinking! Ok, I am in trouble now because my mind can wander sometimes. He laughed again. "I have looked forward to this time with you, Lydia. Your mind always intrigues me," he said so lovingly.

Wait a minute. Jesus couldn't wait to talk *to me*? Now I know I am dreaming.

He said, "Lydia, you are here for answers. I am here to provide those answers. Are you ready?" He gave pause

7

with a look of question, but continued on. "You are about to take a journey that will include you reuniting with loved ones who are anxious to see you. We have much to talk about."

"Tell me why I'm here?" I inquired. With this, we shared a short dialogue of Q&A.

He said, "You have always been in search of me. Your open-mindedness to all possibilities is what brought you here. I knew you would comprehend everything I am going to share with you. The life you are living has dealt some misfortunes but, if you understand your purpose, you will be an advocate for me if and when you return back to your life. You will remember everything you see here, and you may share all you've learned with others. I will guide you with the right words but, first, we must part from your sadness. Your father, brother, and mother are anxious to see you."

"Wow," I said. He had referenced them in the order of their deaths. It had been over 50 years since my father had passed, and almost 30 for my brother. My mother passed more recently, only a couple of years ago. "Are they here now? Are they happy? All three went to heaven?"

"I will let you be the judge of their happiness," He said

in a comforting tone. "We will talk about heaven during your time here."

I then asked the burning question, "Am I dead?"

"That will be up to you. During your journey here, I will address all of your questions. I promise. Now, let us look into the depths of your pain, so that you can begin to see and fully understand," he said as he gave me that loving look I have so quickly grown to covet.

As we walked, he had much to say. His wisdom sang like music for my ears. He began by pointing out that when we pass from earth, our spirit guide appears to escort us. "The light you saw in your room," he told me, "was your Spirit Guide, or Guardian Angel as many call it."

"Does the spirit have a name? Do I call it Light?"

"Yes, the Light has a name. We call the light the Holy Specter (meaning an appearance of something or somebody unexpected or strange derived of the Holy Spirit). It has the same likeness as the Holy Spirit; only, we use Holy Specter so that you will know the difference when we are referencing the Holy Spirit (one of the Trinity) versus the Holy Specter (your Spirit Guide, otherwise known as Guardian Angel). Trust me. It makes it easier to understand when we differentiate one from the other. In essence, they are the same."

"Is the Light a man or a woman?" I asked.

"The Light is what you want it to be," he explained. "It doesn't have to be either one. Male and female are earthly beings. We are in an earthly male form now, so that you are able to relate."

"Ok," I muttered, a little uneasy with the concept of neither male nor female.

"As we continue, it is really important that we address your sadness," he said, taking my hand. With only his touch, my thoughts, memories, and reflections began to come alive. And with his touch, life's adventures, heartbreak and, yes, the pain found themselves by my side. My journey had begun.

3

THE BOTTOM

I had come to a point in life where having faith alone was not working for me anymore, largely, because God's promises were not ringing true for me. Having grown up in the church, much of what I had been told to believe was in conflict with what I was experiencing in life. You know the popular phrases. "I will not forsake you, or when you see only one set of footprints, it was then that I carried you." Does God, I wonder, let us fall to our lowest so he may initiate change in our lives? I don't know. I wish I had all the answers. I am now in my 50's, yet all the dreams I had imagined for my life remains unrealized. My world, it seems, has always been so hostile. People are angry everywhere. Even those guided by their religious beliefs seem angry. Hypocrites, easily comes to mind, but it's not my place to judge. You know, that whole 'judge not lest ye be judged', adage stirs the imagination. Anyway, I try never to hold grudges. If someone offends me, once understanding takes place, I always seek peace. Maybe, I reason, they have their own issues with God's timing and, like me, they are frustrated. As a point of reference, I grew up with a stepfather who beat and verbally abused me. I lived with his violence all through my young life. When he cut me, that was the final nail in the coffin, I left. I left before I ended up *in* a coffin. I had been waiting ever since for the blessings of the Father. Essentially, I've been waiting my entire life. Maybe that was my mistake. I didn't understand enough about God's love to act on it. In the days of my youth, I considered myself a kindred spirit to Joseph. You know the guy with the coat of many colors. Like me, he kept getting beat down, but he never lost his faith or determination. He trusted God completely. In the end, God rewarded him handsomely.

Don't get me wrong. I know God hears my prayers. We have a relationship. If I pray for my daughter, for instance, he's all over it. I can remember one day, a day long ago. We were leaving our home. Our home was on a corner lot where a guard rail separated our land from the road. The neighborhood teens started congregating there to hang out. My daughter, who was about 12 years old at the time, hated it. She said, "Mom, I hate that they sit there. I have to walk by them every day after school."

"Do they pick on you?"

"No, they just stare at me when I walk by."

I said, "Honey, let's pray about it. Let's talk to God about how you are feeling." We prayed riding down the road together. When we came back home, the teens were gone and they never came back. I know it's hard to believe, but it's the truth. The teens who hung out there daily, never congregated there again after that prayer. My heart swelled with love for God. I knew he loved my daughter. I believed all that I read in the Bible, every astounding word. So much so, I used to apply the Biblical stories literally to my own life. If Abraham, for example, laid hands on his sons for blessings, I could do that for my daughter. I even named her after the Son; Christi – Christ and I. I wanted her to always be sheltered by his Grace.

I prayed constantly, it seemed, but the fruition of answered prayers pale in comparison to the volume I delivered. It was my feeling that he should always answer the critical prayers. I'm reminded of Paul. The Bible tells of a weakness/flaw that he had. He prayed that God take it from him. Three times he asked the Lord to remove it. But God said, "My grace is sufficient for you, for my power is made perfect in weakness." Comparing myself to Paul, I am encouraged to know that he is willing to receive my prayers, but I remained humble, happy to know his glory would come at just the right time. This may be my burden. I wanted so desperately to see prayers fulfilled. I listened for his words, however, in the silence, I could not hear them. Was it because the pain was louder than his voice?

One major prayer I desperately wanted answered was for the healing of my mother. At 84, years old she had begun a fast descent into what was soon diagnosed as Alzheimer's. The thought of just how quickly she escalated from moderate symptoms to an unsteady gait, memory loss, and extreme weight loss was shocking. I kept telling her physician the prescribed medicine was making her worse. I did the research and sensed she needed her medication changed. Her physician disagreed. So I insisted on a second opinion. He referred us to a specialist who agreed with him. At first, I accepted the diagnosis in defeat, but something kept me ill at ease. It was breaking my heart seeing my mother this way. She had reverted to childlike behavior; so much so, that our roles were reversed. She was now my child, and I had become the mother. The weight loss began affecting her heart. It became so severe we had to admit her to the hospital more than once. The doctors told the family the prognosis was not good. I could not imagine this happening. Just a few short years ago, mom and I traveled on vacations together where walking all day was undemanding. Now she could barely stand up. Still not satisfied with the diagnosis, I called another hospital and took her to yet another specialist. The new specialist finally gave a diagnosis that made sense. My mother had *hydrocephalus*, fluid on the brain. The specialist immediately referred her to a major hospital to get the fluid drained off to support his diagnosis. Success! She was walking perfectly, back to her normal self, and she stayed that way for days. To remain healthy, the surgeons would need to implant a shunt. We scheduled the operation. I was overjoyed. Finally! She was happy too, but, to our dismay, it was too late. The damage inflicted by the illness had left permanent damage to her body.

On Sunday, two nights before the surgery, she suffered a massive heart attack. She had been staying temporarily in a nursing home for care. The nurses said she would not rest in bed. Frequently, she tried to walk around, stumbling, sometimes losing her balance. I arrived that evening to find her anxious. Rounding the corner to her room, the expression on her face was priceless. Since her decline, she had such innocent expressions on her face. The look of "I need you" was now there. She was sitting in the wheel chair, her small hands kneading the hospital blanket on her lap. She was frail, small, and almost skeletal. I found myself wanting to hug her all the time. I felt she needed my safeguard twenty-four seven. I was almost afraid I would break a bone when I embraced her. That night, as I dressed her for bed, I collapsed into tears. I detested seeing her like this. The long fight to get her healthy had taken its toll. I was with her each and every night.

As I wept, she said, "Don't cry. I have money," as though she assumed I was crying over financial woes. The part about her having money was true. After her passing, we found money stashed all over her house. Don't ask me why that came to her mind, but it did.

I laughed and cried at the same time. I told her, "I'm just sad that you have to go through this." They were sad tears and tears of relief as well. They were tears of joy, too, because on Tuesday she would become whole again. After dressing her for bed, we hugged for a long time. I tucked her into bed and sat beside the bed holding her hand while she fell into slumber. As she lay there, I looked at my mother. She had been a picture of health before, yet, there she lay resting, nearly half the body weight she was mere months ago. I held her hand and I promised her I would not leave until she was asleep. She kept opening her eyes every so often to see if I was still there.

I said, "Mom, I promise I will not leave until you're in dreamland. Just relax, and rest. You need your strength for surgery the day after tomorrow." I cry to this day thinking about that night. It was the last time she spoke. The heart attack she would have later that night, only hours after I left, would affect her speech permanently.

The next morning the nursing home called to tell me they had rushed her to the hospital. They believed she either had a stroke or a heart attack. When I reached the hospital, she was lying there, in a comatose state, just staring into space.

When the doctor came in to speak with me, he said, "She had a massive heart attack." He explained to me in layman's terms that the anterior portion of her heart was no longer operating. Only 9% of her heart was now functioning. She would require a transplant.

I said, "Do it!"

The doctor said, "She would never make it through such an invasive procedure." At her age, they could not operate.

I replied, "I want her transported to the University of Virginia where they may feel differently." He disagreed, but said it was up to me. So, we had her transported to the university.

When the doctors met with the family, the news was largely the same. "We cannot save her. We can only make her comfortable." They began giving her medication that basically put her to sleep. For one week we diligently sat by her side. I left twice that week, long enough to drive home, take a quick shower, and return.

The memory of that final morning still disturbs me. It was 6:05 a.m. I was sitting there holding her hand, as I always had and, instantly, she opened her eyes. She looked at me and began breathing heavily. I yelled for my two brothers and they rushed to her bedside. She looked scared. I said, "We love you so much. You have been a wonderful mother." With that said, a large tear ran down her face. "God wants you with him mom, and it is ok to go. You have lived a love-filled life and God has a beautiful new home for you." A tear rolled down her face again and we locked eyes. All of a sudden, I saw her exit her physical being. A light lifted from within her eyes at 6:10 a.m. I saw the darkness left in its place. It startled my brother, Ron. He fell backwards a little when he saw the light in her eyes exit. He took a deep gasp of breath. He had seen it too. She was dead. Matt, my youngest brother, fell apart. We all, in fact, fell apart. But remembering what I saw when she lifted, I knew life was not over for my mother. It was just beginning.

After telling her it was ok to go, I screamed when it happened. "NO!" I was not ready for her to leave. I had spent the last year caring for her and I would do it forever if needed. All at once, the mother that I had taken care of, was no more. I had no mother. Still holding her hand in mine, I watched as whiteness filled her hands, ran up her arm, and then moved to her precious face. There was stillness in the air. No lifting up and down of her gown from breathing. Only silence, except for the muffled tears from the family. We all yielded to our grief. I couldn't let go of her hand. After a few minutes, I told my brothers that someone should go to the front desk to inform them of her passing. Ron left to let them know. Soon a doctor came in and officially pronounced her deceased at 6:15 a.m. I felt it should have read 6:10 a.m. because that is when she actually passed. Nevertheless, they pronounced the vitals and reported the death at 6:15 a.m. Once calm enough to have a voice again, I called my daughter, Christi, and my sisters. Christi didn't answer my call. I reached my sisters who were devastated by the news. They couldn't decide if it was better to have been there to witness her passing or not. Carly didn't think she could have taken it.

"I know," I said. "It is the hardest thing I have ever done in my life." I hung up and tried calling Christi again. This time she answered. I said to her, "Granny's gone."

"I know," she said. "Granny was just here with me." I couldn't understand what she was trying to say. I assumed she was still groggy since my call would have just woken her.

"Mom, Granny was lying in a bed. She was laid back as if she were on a hospital bed that could lift up, yet there was nothing there to support her. She sat propped up comfortably, as if pure air was holding the weight of her body."

"I asked her, 'Are you dead, Granny?'"

"'Yes, I am honey,' "Granny said to me." 'Come over and sit with me.'"

Christi described how she had climbed onto the bed and arranged herself beside her Grandmother. She sat with her Grandmother's arms wrapped around her.

"Then, I asked Granny, 'Will I ever get to see you again?'"

"Granny replied softly, 'Of course, my love! I will always be with you.'"

"We had a delightful time together mom. I also asked her, 'Granny, what will we do without you?'"

"In her usual comforting tone, she said to me, 'You will be just fine. I will always be near you. I'm not leaving you. I'm just leaving this tired, old body. You will see me again, honey.' "

"That's when I woke up to my phone ringing, and you telling me Granny had died. That's what I meant when I said, 'I know.' She had already been here to tell me."

With that, I knew something miraculous had occurred. Before leaving this earth, my mother had visited my daughter who was hundreds of miles away. Before I could deliver the news of her passing, Christi already knew.

4

REUNION

"Death is difficult to understand," Jesus said upon my return from my mind journey.

"My brother's death was just as devastating," I countered. Then I asked, "How could a loving God allow the tragic drowning of my brother? The call of death is ruthless. I don't think there is anything you could say that would make me understand how his drowning, and finding his body weeks later, could be a lesson to anyone." Then, with an anxious voice, I tearfully added, "My father died when I was only nine years old. I needed him in my life! After he died, the abuse from my stepfather began."

Jesus patiently replied, "That was your brother's burden and his choice to bear. Your father, too, was sad that he left you so soon. Tell me," he said quizzically, "do you think it was easy for me to leave my Father, to live as you live and to die in front of my earthly mother, and heavenly Father? My mother stood below me, watching me suffer. God the Father was watching my pain as well."

I stopped cold. How trivial of me not to realize he

couldn't identify with my grief. "Oh, I am so sorry," I said with great remorse.

"Once you gain clarity of life and its cycle, you will not be so distressed over death. God does not choose the method of your death, but he does allow it," he explained. "Let us resolve the death pain so you may gain a fuller understanding, let go, and take in the rest of your journey." His body suddenly lost the body density and shifted back to light, swirling with sparkles throughout. This time, however, he had a golden glow instead of the pure white light as before. I would soon discover this meant we were entering a new phase level of knowledge. He encircled me just as the Holy Specter enveloped me when I first arrived. It felt dizzying to watch the sparkling light engulf me.

When the light pulled away, I was standing in a meadow. The breeze was blowing gently across the field, joined by a scent of fresh cut grass. "Jesus, where are you?" I asked, somewhat confused. As I looked around, I didn't see him, but I did see a beautiful grand home in the distance. It was the home I had always dreamed of. Expensive, very large, with a lawn manicured to perfection, (so that is where the fresh cut grass smell came from). I stepped from the field onto the trimmed lawn, and shouted out loud, "Ah, not a crab grass in sight! This must be heaven." I smiled to myself. My own house was built on the edge of a field and I fought crab grass constantly. So, this was an enormous feat in my eyes since it, too, was at the edge of a gorgeous meadow. The grass was the darkest green I had ever encountered. Each blade had a depth to it, as if you could reach inside its color. As I walked on it, I looked back over my steps to see blades return upright the minute my foot was removed, as if they were following me, leaving no indication I had ever stepped there. A floral scent caught my attention, inviting me to look toward the edge of the house where flowers were positioned all along its base. They directed themselves toward me as I approached, as if just for my pleasure. I wondered what would happen if someone else were here with me. Could they turn two different directions at the same time? "H-e-l-l-o, this is Heaven. Anything is possible," I said out loud as I cautiously laughed.

I began to climb the beautiful steps of stone. They were tan stones, with tinges of beige and small brown specs on them. Oh, so exquisite. I walked up keeping my eye on the massive door ahead of me. As I approached the top of the steps and the porch landing, I searched for the doorbell, but saw none. I knocked and stood there waiting, but no one came. I turned the door knob and the door opened. I walked into the grand foyer and looked around at the splendor before my eyes. The chandelier was stunning, full of beautiful lighting and crystals - so luminous. "Hello," I said, wondering if I should have just walked in. Jesus wanted me here. I knew that much. However it looked like no one was home. I beheld a beautiful stair case and wondered if anyone was within earshot of this big house.

Suddenly, a well-dressed man entered the foyer from a door off to my left. As he approached, I saw he was the same elderly man who lived across the hall from mom's room at the nursing home. He was well now and no longer in need of a wheelchair. He must have died to be here, I thought. He used to sit in the hallway outside of my mother's room. When he would see me coming down the hall, he would say, "Here comes your daughter, Ms. Cantor." He announced us every time. So our family started calling him the butler. He loved it when we called him that, such a nice man.

"Welcome, Miss. We have been expecting you," he said formally.

I asked, mystified, "Who is expecting me?"

"The family of the manor of course," he said with a

smile. "Please permit me to take you to the parlor where the family will join you shortly," he said, still smiling.

"Ok," I said, following behind him to my right. I asked, "Do you remember me?"

"Certainly," he said. Still smiling, he added, "You brought me candy for Easter. I was touched by your kindness and was given the honor of being your greeter in this part of your journey."

"Yes. Yes I did," I said as I recalled. I had forgotten all about that candy. I remembered him in a special way, as a protector of my mother. He would inform me of any comings and goings of the day with her, even the nurses.

We entered an enormous room holding two bold, white couches. The color scheme of the room was one of stark contrast between black and white. Vibrant, black table lamps were placed on black end tables standing on either side of the couches. The tables had the tiniest white specks, in perfect contrast to the solid black lamps. There was a large black and white rug beneath the white couches. Not a bold black and white contrast, but two colors that mingled ever so gently to complement the couches skillfully, as if caressing their legs so perfectly placed. Both couches were facing each other. At each end were two large, black, Queen Ann chairs. They, too, had the tiniest of white specs in the material. It was a stunning room. The picture that hung over the enormous white mantel appeared to have a white light beaming and dancing over a black background. The light seemed to move in sync with my movements. I looked away and back again to be sure I was seeing it clearly. As I sat down, the Gentleman announced the family would be with me soon. I thanked him, and he exited the room.

I took this short time to look around the room for pictures, clues, or anything to identify the family that I would soon meet. I imagined it could be Joseph. From the days of my youth Joseph and his coat of many colors has been a favorite Bible story. I searched the room for telltale hints of who lived there. The only evidence I found in the room was a picture of ME! I stood and walked directly to the quaintly decorated table where my picture sat as the centerpiece. Heaven was validated again! I hate having my picture taken and, under no circumstance would I have ever allowed this! I never thought of myself as photogenic but, for once, this was a good picture, in fact it was great. I looked happy in the picture, and young. Wow! I must find out who took this picture. I'd pay high dollar for him/her to capture my essence like that again in a portrait for my home.

At that moment, the large main door began to open. I turned toward it and eagerly looked to see the mystery family. I was stunned! It was my mother and father! They were holding hands as they entered the room. My mother was young and beautiful. She looked just like the picture I have of her in her twenties on my desk at work. My dad looked tall, young, and handsome. They were grinning from ear to ear, looking at me, then looking back to each other. Their gazes to each other were so full of love. I smiled and wanted to cry. I was so happy.

Mom ran over and grabbed me. Tears of happiness flowed without restraint. We hugged, and we hugged some more.

Dad said, "Can I get in on this love fest?" I grabbed him and cried into his chest. It was then that I smelled the Old Spice cologne he used to wear.

"Oh, Daddy," I said in a little girl's voice. I felt as if I were his little girl again.

"Hi, Baby," he said with a hoarseness in his voice that told me he was ready to cry too. "I have missed you so much. Let me take a look at you. You have grown into a beautiful woman, honey. When we were told we would get to see you, we were so happy." Just then, Mom got back into the hug with us.

"Let's sit down and talk," Mom said. The three of us sat on one of the white couches.

"This place is a dream," I said looking around the room. "Mom, you finally received the mansion you deserved."

"Oh, this ol' place," she teased. "Actually, this is *your* heavenly place honey. When you're in heaven, all is perfect. This is your dream home, and this is your decorating style. We are here with you in your perfect world."

"I don't understand," I said, now totally confused. "Why am I not visiting you in your perfect world? By the way, what would that be?"

She laughed and said, "This house is a little too grand for me. I have simpler tastes. In heaven you can be in more than one place at a time. For you, I am in human form, but I can be in any form I desire. I can be here and there at the same time. I am not limited to the earthly body's restricted movements. I am in a form now that you desire and need to see. I am healthy and happy, just as I was in the picture on your desk. I can also be older if you need that."

Without me saying, "I need that," she turned into the healthy person she was right before she became sick, only one year before her death. I was astounded. "Oh, mom," I said grabbing her at the same time. "Mom, tell me about your death. I need to know if your passing was traumatic."

"When I left my body, my Holy Specter arrived and gave me immediate peace," she said. "When you first die, all previous memories of heaven are not there. That is why the Holy Specter is there to meet you. Once here, you are re-acclimated to your perfect heaven. In most cases, that means you go through the heavenly process of reviewing the life you just left. You go before God, with Jesus sitting at his right hand, along with the Holy Spirit. You tell him what you gained or lost from your experience. Of course, he already knows. This is for your benefit. Then you are given your new status. If you gained from your life, your color will change. If you did not learn from your life, you either stay the same or go to repair. I understand you will be going on a journey to see these things."

"So, Dad, did you go through the same thing?"

"Yes, honey I did," he said.

"Are you happy here?"

"We both are," they said in unison.

30

Dad continued, "Here, each person has their own perfect life. Your perfect life is that your mother and I are together. So we are in *your* heaven. Part of our heavenly bodies stay with you while the other parts of ourselves are doing other heavenly things of perfection. For instance, I may be a mentor for other souls, or your mother and I are together in our own paradise. Heaven is all about perfection for you and, of course, God."

"So, you have the ability to be dispersed in different forms, in different locations at the same time," I said, completely understanding the concept. All of my afterlife studying is sure paying off. "How cool is that?"

I happened to glance at the decorated table with my picture on it. Now, Dad and Mom's picture was there, seemingly smiling at me. I walked over to check it out. They were arm in arm, smiling at the camera. They had a happy, contented look on their faces, too. "So, how long do we get to stay together?"

"We aren't sure, but we have another surprise for you," Mom said.

"What could be better than this?" I asked, believing every word.

"W-e-l-l," she said. They were both smiling at each

other.

At that moment, the door opened. In walked my brother, Chad. I couldn't contain myself. I ran to him with pure excitement! It was so overwhelming. He had that mischievous smile on his face. You see, he was the jokester of the family, and he always had that "up to something grin." I turned back to Mom and Dad and asked, "Have you guys been together this whole time?" They nodded yes, unable to speak from being choked up.

"Lydia, I know it has been hard on you losing us but, trust me, we came to a better place. We are so happy here. It is much better than the earthly world."

Chad led me back over to the couch, and we sat between Mom and Dad. The couch seemed to shift into a U shape so we could better see each other.

Emotionally charged, I said, "Chad, you can't know our devastation when we couldn't find your body for two weeks. It killed me to know you were lying out there somewhere alone and hurt."

"Lydia, that's just it. The minute I drowned, I was lifted to meet my Holy Specter. The body left out there for two weeks did not have me in it any longer. I lived the life I was supposed to live, and I died at the appropriate time.

We all choose life, but we know death follows life eventually. There is no getting around that. Once you are here, and you have your memory restored, you are so glad to be home. Heaven is home, Lydia, not earth. We all choose to go to earth in order to learn and grow. In the heavenly realm, you are protected from hurt and pain."

With that confirmation, I glanced toward the table. Now Chad's picture had appeared. I laughed. I embraced Chad, and I didn't want to let him go. I was so happy to see all of them.

"So, what will happen now?" I asked, hoping it wouldn't mean separation from them.

"We are told we can answer any questions you have. What do you want to know?"

I began with this long list of questions. "Will we be together when I die? Have you been with or seen God face to face? What does he look like? What do you do in heaven?"

"Whoa," Chad said while giving me the bear hug. "Ok, first question. Will we be together when you die? Yes, if that is your perfect heaven."

"Well, of course, it is." I said, matter of fact.

"Have you been with or seen God face to face?" repeating the second question. "Yes, all souls go through a judgment after their return from life's experience."

"What does God look like?"

"He looks different to each soul. Each soul projects its light into him differently. Our souls blend with his. He is in us, around us, and through us."

I found it strange that I got that, but I did. "So what do you do on a daily basis?"

"Right now, I am reviewing and preparing for the next life I will be living and learning from," Chad answered.

I asked, "Is this similar to reincarnation?"

"Yes and no," Dad said. "We get the option to choose from selected lives that are shown to us. We watch excerpts of about 4 lives. We don't know the outcome of those lives, but we choose based on the lessons a particular life will teach us."

"Wow! I hope I get the chance to see that while I'm here," I said in a hopeful tone.

"What we want you to understand now," Mom said, "is that death is not the end. It is sad that we part, yes. We will miss each other, but we will be together again. It all has a purpose. You soon will be back in your perfect world, and we will be together again. So, lose the lost feeling, and stop letting it affect your journey in this life. You have a mission and purpose in every life you choose, so live it to the fullest. You don't want to get back here to discover you wasted the gift of life."

"I understand," I said, somewhat ashamed that I had held on to the pain so much. "The loss of you guys hurt so much. The emptiness I felt when you left was unbearable."

Mom said, "Lydia, I felt the same way over losing Chad at such a young age. Don't you remember? I couldn't speak of him without crying? Reuniting with him here was such a joy." She leaned over and kissed his cheek, then mine.

Chad said, "You should see us in light form, Lydia. We have so much fun. Dancing around and moving into each other. We feel one another's emotions. Feelings are not as one dimensional as we sometimes think. When the Holy Spirit merges with you, it is the most wonderful feeling that overcomes you. You become so much more intensified. Happiness makes you glow brighter. Feelings of love are bursting. Understanding is complete. You know how the other person is feeling so you get lost in all of the emotions."

All of a sudden the three looked anxious. Dad said, "We are told it is time to go."

Mom repeated, "We are told it is time to go. Then said, take with you this time together and know that we are happy. Know, too, that all is as it should be for now. We love you."

With that, each one embraced me as their bodies became a swirling light that encircled me, and then left the room, leaving me with warmth, love, and a whole new memory of them. They left me with the understanding that God will judge us not according to what we endured, but according to how much we have loved.

5

REPAIR STATION

I stood there after my family departed feeling elated that I had spent the time with them. Now knowing that they were happy made a big difference. I walked to the table again. Each picture brought me great joy as they smiled back at me. I felt so much warmth emanating from them. What they shared made me see things differently. I now knew I had to let go of their traumatic deaths, and move on. I would see them again, maybe sooner than I thought. Jesus did say that it would be my choice to stay or go. Not letting myself think of my daughter, Christi, my mind was telling me, "Stay here."

I gazed at the pictures, deep in thought. Out of the corner of my eye, I noticed a reflection of light dancing on the walls. I turned around to find Jesus taking shape again. Once formed, the light radiated only from the edges of his skin as before. He asked if I felt soothed now that I had learned of my family's well-being. I embraced him and thanked him so much for the gift. While in his embrace, I felt his love fill me everywhere. The joy I was feeling was indescribable. I wanted to laugh, cry, dance, and sing all at once with an overwhelming joy.

He asked, "Are you ready to continue with your journey?"

"Yes," I said. "More than ready."

At once, he began the transition to a light being and surrounded me. When we stopped what seemed to be traveling, we were back to where we were when I first met him. There was a sense of nothingness. I looked, but didn't see anything. From here, he began to explain the process of heaven.

"In a moment," Jesus said, "you will see Mr. Smith arrive. Mr. Smith has just passed away on earth. His actions on earth harmed many and his soul has been damaged. When he approaches, you will see what his choices have done to his soul."

At that moment, Mr. Smith emerged. I was placed a small distance away and felt he should be able to see me, but he didn't show any sign of detection, nor did he acknowledge me. He was simply standing there, just as I did when I first arrived. As I watched him, I noticed a light energy approaching him, a likeness to the light that approached me upon my arrival. It began to dance around him but, clearly, it was not as playful as it had been with me. The light suddenly backed away. Instead of caressing him, the light became a bright beam shining toward him. As the light touched Mr. Smith's body, he became a light as well. I noticed however, this man's light had dark spots throughout its light stream, instead of all of the sparkles I had witnessed in other light entities.

I asked Jesus, "What are the dark spots? Why doesn't he have the sparkles?"

"His light has been damaged by the darkness he participated in on earth. When a soul arrives with a light deficiency, they are routed immediately for repair and restoration. We need to mend his soul before he can go back into the normal heavenly realm," Jesus explained.

At that moment, the man was led away. As they began to disappear, I realized we had moved, too. We had followed him to an area where there were men who looked like doctors or technicians, dressed in white robes. Mr. Smith was immediately directed by one of the robed men to move under a dome where he was sealed and locked down. Precipitously, another light merged with his light inside the dome. You could tell the difference between the two lights because of the gray hues associated with his color. Within his light I could still see the dark spots. Next, the scene resembled a battle episode of *Star Trek,* or the movie, *Star Wars*. Something began shooting. Bright fire spots erupted as they hit the dark spots. This light object kept circling within the dome in search of the spots. The spots were moving around, not as if trying to get away but, more precisely, like they were being shaken into position for fire. There were rapid fires and explosive eruptions until the circling light began to slow and came to a stop. At completion, there were no dark spots left, and the gray colors were gone.

Jesus explained, "The soul's spirit has now been repaired. The Holy Spirit has entered the soul's light and destroyed the damaged emitters. As you saw, the dark lights disappear. This means the man's soul has been renewed. This man chose a lesson that gave him a choice of good or evil. Unfortunately, he and the body he selected chose evil. In his earth life, he murdered innocent people through his own devious motivations."

"What a terrible person," I said, somewhat afraid the bad soul could escape or get near me. I wondered if the dark spots could affect me if I were too close. I caught myself physically moving backward, to avoid any contact with him as he emerged from the dome.

Jesus, of course, knew my thoughts and placed his arm around me. "Don't be concerned. The evil has been extracted and exiled. He will now rejoin the normal process for soul assessment. He will review the life he just left. His journey is decidedly different than most normal returns. With a normal return, a soul is allowed to select their next life. A damaged soul loses that option. His future life will be *chosen* for him. In this case, because his life was full of mayhem and he chose to murder, he will be required to become a murdered *victim*. He will experience the trauma of *being* murdered and face the terror and fear his previous life imposed on others. That is how he would make his way back to becoming whole again. This journey will be a difficult one to endure. The adage, *'you reap what you sow,'* applies here."

I asked, "Does he still remember what he did now that he has been purged?"

"Yes. He will feel remorse for his actions. As he reviews the results of his behaviors, he will break down psychologically, now having seen the hurt and pain he has caused for his victims and their families. He will have much to answer to," Jesus said.

"How can he be here in Heaven when he has done such unforgiveable things?"

Jesus answered clearly, "God is a loving God. He gives

everyone a choice to be with him. There are some who will always choose not to stay here in heaven. When that occurs, they will be cast into darkness never to return. Everyone is a child of God. He will always love you and want you with him, but it is always your choice. Those who came back and felt remorse for their behavior learned a lesson in self-discipline and, of course, experienced the repercussions for their actions. They now know firsthand the outcome of evil and how their separation from God is a disconcerting place to be. Most will never get that close to evil again. Let's return to your question of doing such an unforgiveable thing. My life and death made forgiveness possible. Show repentance, ask, and you will receive. It is just that simple. Love will always be your redeemer."

I asked, "What will happen to him now?"

"He will review his life and then go before judgment."

Which begged another question: "Will that be where it is decided whether he goes to heaven or hell?"

"No, that was decided when he arrived. As the Holy Spirit put the light beam on him, he could refuse to accept the light and go into darkness. He accepted repair and now will review the choices he made in the life he just left. He will examine how he became a murderer, how his horrible life with an abusive parent led to his pent up anger and rebellion, and how he wanted others to hurt like he'd been hurt."

"He has a difficult time ahead of him on his return to earth. To live the life of being murdered will be overwhelming for him, almost unbearable. Yet, when he returns, the depth of his knowledge and the extent of this growth will be evident. He can become a great teacher with this experience. His choices will never be the same after his next life. He will make wiser, more inspiring choices going into future lives or divine missions. You will see his aura change color as his soul is nurtured. That is why I came to earth as man. I wanted to know your agony, your struggles, and your happiness as an earth-bound human. I wanted to experience the challenges humans face firsthand. That is why I grew to love you and to become a sacrifice for all souls. I chose that life just as Mr. Smith chose his own."

I find this whole process intriguing. I thought going to heaven was only for the good and those who sin without salvation were doomed to hell fire. I could only come to a more complete understanding through the help of Jesus, and not through my own understanding. With his help, I no longer saw Mr. Smith as a horrible person but, instead, as a misguided, wounded human. The rage he must have felt from his childhood spilled over to innocent victims who fell prey to his injured soul. I, too, experienced that rage myself from an abuser. The difference between us may be in the end. I chose not to take out my hurt and pain on others; instead, I chose love. With this new insight, I can see how I would empathize with others, even with a murderer. Viewing this soul through my former self would have never allowed me to indulge in perfect understanding, or comprehend my love for him. Rather, I would have thought him vile and ruthless, deserving punishment to the maximum extent possible. It reminds me of the story of the thief, crucified with Jesus, who had asked Jesus to remember him when he came unto his kingdom. Doing so, he was told, "Today you will be with me in Paradise." It also reminds me of the quote from Martin Luther King Jr.; "as my sufferings mounted, I soon realized that there were two ways in which I could respond to my situation; either to react with bitterness or seek to transform the suffering into a creative force. I decided to follow the latter course."

With that thought, the swirl began again and, in an instant, we were back to the entrance point, the first location where there was nothingness. I could not in my wildest dreams imagine what was waiting for me next.

6

DEPTHS OF DARKNESS

Jesus asked, "Now, do you understand the process of an injured soul?"

I said, "I think so, but if killing doesn't send you to hell, what can a person do that is so unforgiveable?"

"The person that refuses the Light when he arrives is separated from God. With a fully darkened soul, he is destined for a life in darkness instead of a life in the heavenly realm. By rejecting the Light, he rejects the Holy Spirit."

Jesus continued, "A person that commits the same murders as Mr. Smith, but with no remorse would be another example of unforgiveness. Someone who cares nothing for others and offers no love, and has no redeeming qualities is another example, in essence they turn from light to darkness."

"Geez, sounds like my ex," I thought.

Jesus smiled and shot me a cocked eyebrow look. "Funny," he said.

Oops, I forgot he could read my mind. "WELL." I laughed.

Jesus said, "For this next lesson, turn and look to where Mr. Smith arrived before."

I turned to look and a man was just entering the area. At once, I felt a force pulling us quickly backwards and a dome soon enveloped us. I panicked and started yelling, "What's happening?"

"You are now seeing someone who has not accepted the light," Jesus said. "Just watch," he said while nodding his head in the direction of the man.

The light entity began approaching the man just as it had done for both me and Mr. Smith. Only this time, as it approached, it stopped (the same as it did with Mr. Smith) and the light became a beam. Instead of the man turning into light, like Mr. Smith with his dark spots, this man instantly turned into a dark being resembling dark smoke. It grew large and ugly as it focused on rejecting the light. I could feel the dark emotions and the pull of the man's rebellion. There was anger and hate radiating from him. Before long, I heard bellowing, blood curdling screams, similar to those terrifying screams you might hear at Halloween or in a horror movie. The light stream backed away. Suddenly, it was in the dome with us.

The area around the dark being was now darkening as well. I heard crying, wailing, and a mean, vicious laugh. I looked at Jesus. He had such a sad look on his face. Not fear as I had expected; nor like I felt but, rather, true sadness was in his eyes. I was sure I saw a tear trickle down his face, or was it falling from my eyes? I couldn't tell.

Dark hands and arms in human form were reaching up around the man's feet and legs. He was petrified, and so was I. He started screaming and, as he did, the darkness began rising to envelop him. He was fighting and cursing the darkness, but the darkness overcame his attempts to resist. Suddenly, the floor gave way and he began falling, flailing and grabbing as he went. I was so scared I grabbed Jesus and laid my head on his chest, turning to watch with one eye.

Then, it was over. The man was gone and so was the darkness. The area was back to nothingness again. The dome that covered us vanished as quickly as it had appeared.

"Wow," was all I could get out of my mouth. Stunned, I felt my heart pounding out of my chest.

"I know," Jesus said. "It breaks my heart. He did not

have to go this far. Sacrifices were made so he would not have to be separated, but he did not accept me. It saddens me to witness it."

I asked, "So, this is what happens when someone chooses darkness over light?"

"Yes," Jesus replied.

"Well you can bet I won't make that mistake," I said with a sigh. I had no idea it was like that.

Jesus said, "No one truly realizes the devastating reality of choosing darkness."

I asked, "Will you allow me to write about this?"

"Yes, you have my permission, I want you to share your time here with the world."

With this, my thoughts returned to my daughter again. I hope she's ok, but I must not think about her right now.

Jesus smiled knowing my thoughts. "You will know when it is time," he said with tenderness.

"Jesus, have I said I love you yet?" I smiled at him and I wanted to put a big ol' bear hug on him, but I refrained.

He laughed so hard. I thought he was in hysteria.

I asked, "What's so funny?"

"After everything you have witnessed, you still go back to love. You make me happy," he said.

"I am so overwhelmed and filled with joy to be here with you. I will always cherish this time with you," I replied warmly.

"I feel the same," he said genuinely. The warmth in his eyes told me I was precious to him.

"Ok, on with your journey," he said. "Next, you will witness a normal entry with no repair or darkness. I will depart from you now. Your Holy Specter will guide you through the normal process."

"Oh, don't leave," I said wanting ardently for him to stay.

"I am not leaving you. I am always with you. All you need to do is feel me. We are one."

With that, he was gone. I was left standing there like a new arrival.

7

GUESS WHO'S COMING TO DINNER?

The Holy Specter sat me down in the location at the entrance point where Mr. Smith, myself, and the dark man had arrived previously. The light was coming toward me, as before, dancing and swirling around me. I smiled now, knowing more about the process. I couldn't wait to see what would happen next. The light entity formed itself into human shape and introduced itself.

"Hello, Lydia. My name is Lambrett (meaning light of land). I am your greeter for this part of your journey. I greet all who enter this realm to assist with their entry. Some continue on a normal journey, others repair, and there are those who reject the light. I prevent anyone from going further if they need repair, or choose to reject. This does not apply to you. We, of course already know your status from your earlier arrival. Your Holy Specter will guide you through your journey from this point."

I looked toward my Specter as it was developing into human form. As previously, it had a light glowing around the edges of its skin. I have found now that the glow is on everyone who is in this realm. A smiling man appeared. I had no recollection of him, but I felt I knew him. It was like seeing an old friend, a reunion of sorts. I didn't recognize him, however, as anyone from my life.

Looking at him, I said, "Do I know you? I feel as though we've met."

"Yes, and no. I am your Guardian Angel. I have never left your side," he says with a personal intimacy that I still felt I knew. "I am referred to as Specter when you pass from one life to another. That is when I show my light to you. As your Guardian Angel, you cannot see me, but many times you have felt me."

"So, it is true. We do have a Guardian Angel?"

"Yes, most definitely," he said with conviction and with a humble heart.

I looked back at Lambrett. He bows to me and announces my journey. "You will now go to your *return* celebration. Just take your Specter's hand and he will guide you."

I asked, turning toward the Holy Specter, "Is your name Specter? Or is it more like a title, the Holy Specter?"

"You may call me Specter. I answer to many things," he said with a smile.

I held my hand out to his, and the minute we touched he began circling as in the previous journeys. We landed in the yard of the house I had been to earlier. This time, instead of seeing no one there, we were met by an enormous amount of people and unfamiliar beings. Approaching through the yard holding Specter's hand, fireworks started going off. There was yelling and dancing and celebrating as I approached.

I asked Specter, "What are they celebrating?"

"You," he said with a grin.

"Me?"

"Yes, they are celebrating your return. It is always a celebrated event when a loved one returns."

We walked past everyone going up the steps to the house. People were grabbing me and hugging me. I looked at them, but I didn't know any of them. They acted as though they were so happy to see me *again*.

"I asked Specter, "How do I know them?"

He said, "Many from past lives. It will all come back

to you when you properly pass over."

Reaching the top landing on the porch, the door opened as we approached. Walking inside, Specter led me to the left instead of to the right as before. When we walked into the room, there was an enormous table. It had a black wood grain top with matching chairs. The seating and center of the backs of the chairs were padded with white cushioned cloth that looked like you could lose yourself in comfort. There were too many chairs to count. They just went on and on. It was beautifully decorated. It had white sparkling placemats all along the table. The silver was placed meticulously alongside expensive china. Clear crystal goblets were strategically placed by each plate, except for one place setting. There I saw a tattered, wooden goblet, something you might see at the table of the poorest among poor. The Specter told me that goblet belongs to Jesus. He is always here, even when his presence is not seen. The goblets were each filled half way with what I assumed to be red wine. The center pieces, which consisted of stems of white sparkling balls and baby's breath, combined with beautiful red bloomed flowers were placed strategically in vases all the way down the table. The flower wasn't a rose, nor was it a carnation. I had never seen this flower before. It was as if a rose and a carnation had been interwoven. The layers and texture of the flowers were distinctly different, but blended exquisitely. I walked to the table and leaned over to smell the aroma. The fragrance was delightful, filling my senses with the scent of sweet perfume.

"Stunning," I said to Specter. "Absolutely stunning."

I noticed movement from the corner of my eye. From the farthest reaches of the room, light beings began dropping from the ceiling. The room was soon dancing with emitting light entities that were warm and happy. Beautiful music began playing from somewhere. I looked but couldn't find the source. I loved the melody. It was infectious. I wanted to hum it.

Once the lights began to take on the human forms, I could see my mom, dad, and brother were there. They came over at once to embrace me.

I asked, "Did you know we would get to see each other again?"

"No," mom said. "This is a wonderful surprise."

My Specter interjected that I will see many who had gone before me. It was at that time that a little boy ran up to me yelling, "Nunna"!

I couldn't believe my eyes. It was my aunt's little boy

who had drowned at four years old. When I was 12 years old, I used to baby sit for them. Jeffrey could not say my name when he was two, so he always called me Nunna. It stuck. He continued the name even at four years old. I loved that little boy so much. He had brown hair, cut in the famous Beatle style haircut that framed the biggest brown eyes you'd ever seen. He could have easily been a child model. He was so cute. I picked him up and hugged him as if I had last seen him just yesterday. Kissing his little cheeks made him giggle with joy.

Jeffrey had drowned in a horrible flood that ripped apart a whole community. In the middle of the night, the rivers exceeded their banks. Their house came crashing down in a pillage of destruction. It took days to find his little body. The loss was devastating to his mother and father. His mother was never the same again. Jeffrey's death deadened her emotions and trust in life.

Jeffrey said, bringing me back to the moment, "Guess who's here?"

"Who?" I couldn't begin to guess who it could be.

"Poochie!" he yelled.

"Where?" I said with more excitement than I could contain. Poochie was my little hound dog. I had been given Poochie as a puppy, and we had an undeniable bond. She went everywhere with me, always by my side. I was devastated when my stepfather put her in the trunk of his car and hauled her away.

The neighbor's dog was mean. When the postman came to deliver the mail, she would try to break free of the restraints to attack him. Poochie on the other hand, would stand in our yard and bark. She never bothered the postman, but the post office sent a letter stating we had to restrain her or fines would ensue. Instead of restraining her, my stepfather decided to get rid of her. I cried so hard I wanted to die when he pulled away that night with her in the trunk. She was my family. Actually, she was closer than my family, she was mine, part of my soul. To this day, my heart breaks over that dog.

I looked at Specter. "Is she here?"

Suddenly, I heard a clicking sound of toenails and feet running on the floor. Poochie ran to me and jumped up on me. She was jumping up and down trying to get closer to me. I was hugging and kissing her on the head and trying to get her to stand still so we could properly embrace. She was exactly the same! "Poochie! Poochie, my sweet baby!"

My heart was bursting with joy. Jeffrey was rubbing

her and kissing her on the head, too. Specter was watching in delight as we played with her.

In the midst of our reunion, I felt a hand lay on my back as I leaned over rubbing Poochie. I looked up to see my grandfather (my dad's dad) standing there. Dad was beside him, both smiling at me. I hugged my grandpa with much the same enthusiasm as Poochie showed seeing me.

Next, an elderly lady and a gentleman walked up to me and said, "We are your mother's mother and father." I looked at mom who was now crying. She always did that. When I used to come home from school, she would be crying and emotional over a soap opera. This was a great reason to cry now though, so, I smiled at her and laughed.

We all embraced and I said, "I am so happy to meet you." They died before I was old enough to know them. My mother's mother died giving birth to one of my mother's siblings. I embraced each one and I looked at mom's mother. Wow, it was easy to see the resemblance. I could see more of the Indian heritage in my grandmother, than I saw in my mom. It was definitely clear she had native blood lines.

Everyone started gathering near the table. It looked as if everyone knew their place and began seating themselves appropriately. Specter motioned to the seat at the end of the table. I walked over to the chair and waited while Specter pulled it out to seat me. Poochie, who was not leaving my side, had been standing beside me the whole time. Now she followed me to the chair, and as I was seated, she sat beside me.

What had previously been quiet (while everyone took their turn giving me hugs) was now a bustle of rumbling voices and laughter. Containers of food began appearing on the table. Each was placed randomly on the table within everyone's reach. The food smelled deliciously appetizing. I didn't recognize one item in the containers. Some looked like fruit, some like vegetables. I saw something that resembled rice, but had the flavor of a potato. Everyone it seemed, joyously helped themselves and talked non-stop during the whole meal. It felt like Christmas with the gathering of family and friends. Mom and dad sat next to me along with Chad and Jeffrey. I couldn't help but think about Christi and how I wish she were here. It would be the most perfect day if the rest of my family could be here, too. I know my sister would love to see dad and, of course, mom and Chad too.

I looked down the table and next to mom's mom and dad was my aunt Lidia. I was named after her. She went by

Liddy for short. Our names were the same but, spelled differently. She smiled at me, got out of her chair, and came over to kiss me on the cheek. She said, "thank you for fixing my hair for my funeral." After my aunt's death, my cousin called to ask if I would consider doing her mother's hair at the funeral home. Of course I said yes.

"You knew that?"

"Yes, and I looked wonderful!" We both died laughing. She returned to her seat as everyone continued talking and having the time of their lives. At least it seemed that way to me.

I sat there experiencing pure happiness as I looked down the table. Every time I looked at a new face, a new memory came alive. I saw an old childhood friend that had died in her teens in a car accident. Then, I saw Brad, the man I was engaged to, when I was in my late twenties. Brad was in the Air force and had died in a plane crash. I jumped up, ran to him, and just held his face in my hands. "I still love you," I said.

"I still love you," he said while tears were welling up in his eyes.

It was as if we were still a couple. My feelings, just as strong as they were back then, confused me, having had so much time elapsed after his passing. A poignant lesson for me in this celebration is that love never dies.

We all ate, reminisced of old times, and talked of our adventures. It was exhilarating to see how each person would be beside me at any given moment to talk without any of us moving an inch. If the conversation was between Brad and me, he was next to me. If the conversation was with my brother, Chad, he was there. Everyone was within reach. All I had to do was think of them, and they were in front of me. What a joy this marvelous heaven is.

As dinner ended, everyone came by to say their goodbyes. I hugged each person having never felt so much love in my life. To think this was all for me. Each person exited the same way they came, except Poochie. She was not leaving my side. She had sat beside me the whole time, eating her meal as I ate my own.

The departure was bittersweet. I had a heavy heart as each left. I would need to make the decision to return to earth or stay to see them again. My heart was heavy with the sadness of their departure, but somehow at peace, too.

My Specter led me back out to the entryway of the house. The Gentleman from the nursing home said he would lead me to my quarters. We walked up the huge staircase and into a stunning master suite. Poochie still at my feet, followed me up the stairs. The room was decorated with matching bedding, lamp shades, and large rugs on the beautiful hardwood floors. A cozy fire was blazing in the fireplace. It had a soothing dimness that told me night had set in. I walked to the window to see the sun setting over an open meadow. There was a concrete balcony that I walked out on while taking in the night breeze. The air was fresh and crisp with just enough coolness to warrant the fire in the fireplace. The smell of honeysuckle filled the air as I stood there embracing the moment.

"Thank you God, Jesus, and Holy Spirit for this awesome adventure."

As I came back into the room, the gentleman said he was retiring for the night, and he would see me in the morning. I thanked him as he departed.

I walked over to the bed and picked up a beautiful flowing night gown in wait for me. I found the bathroom, took a long luxurious bath, and piled into the plush bed. Poochie jumped up on the bed and got cozy on her own side. I looked at her puppy dog face and said "I love you." With an inquiring expression as well, I added, "I hope heavenly dogs are potty trained." I laughed giving her a big rub.

As I lay there, I repeated my spoken words earlier, "What a joy this marvelous heaven is." I finished my prayers and began falling asleep. "I knew I wanted to stay."

8

DE'JA VU

I woke early the next morning to find a cold nose pressed against my cheek. Poochie was still by my side nudging me to wake up. Feeling refreshed and rested, I rolled onto my back, thinking I might find everything had been a dream. To my delight, I was still in the beautiful master suite I had retired in. I stretched, and relaxed as I thought about events of the night before. It was wonderful to see those again who had passed or crossed over before me. The love in the room was infectious. The night was brimming with love, happiness, and wonderful music.

Poochie was lying there patiently waiting for me to get up. I looked at her and asked, "Would you like to be fed?"

She looked at me as if she understood the question and gave a little, "Gruff."

I jumped out of bed and walked to the balcony to see the rising sun almost at its peak. The breeze was blowing through the drapes that I had pulled before retiring the night before. The views, the smells, and the peaceful feelings I had enjoyed that morning would soon be replaced by my emotional attachment to the trauma my life had offered, not to mention the rage I had long forgotten.

After a quick shower, Poochie and I headed down stairs to seek nourishment for this newfound, beautiful body. I had returned to my youth of the twenties.

We went to the dining area of last night's event only to find it empty. I walked back to the foyer in the entry area and found Specter just entering.

"Good morning," he said very cheerfully.

"And a good morning to you as well," I said.

He asks, "How did you sleep?"

"Heavenly." I smiled at the choice of my word.

He smiled as well. "Let's take a walk," as he motioned toward the front door.

We walked out into the front yard and Poochie immediately took off running. She disappeared somewhere around the house as my Holy Specter and I continued out through the yard at a casual stroll, enjoying the beautiful morning.

"When we return we will have breakfast, then continue with your eventful day."

I asked, "Do you know what happens today?"

"I do, but each process is different depending on the subject," he said.

Did I notice a look of concern on that warm face, I thought? I shrugged it off by thinking of the wonderful things that had happened so far. I had begun to develop trust in the place I called Heaven.

We had made a complete walk around the grounds, when we turned to enter the house again. Specter and I went in and had breakfast together. Poochie enjoyed a feast of her own as well. As I watched her eat, all the love and warmth I had for her when I was a child still burned strongly in this old heart of mine. I sensed she was anxious not wanting to be very far from me. I am finding it so hard to believe she remembers me. Our love was a strong one for sure.

After breakfast, we went down a flight of stairs toward the back of the house and entered a room that looked like a library. Along each wall were shelves full of books. I walked over to read the covers of the books on one of the shelves. One of them had engraved initials on the outside of it. LSM 06-04-1955. Oh my, I thought, that's my birthday! I looked at the Holy Specter who was watching me.

"By the look on your face, I can see you have found your book."

"Yes," I said a little excited. "May I open it?"

In that moment, a light form began to appear. It was so brilliant. I had to turn my head as it placed itself right in front of me. Once set, the light began to materialize into the human form, but this time there was a clear essence. I could see him, yet, I could see through him at the same time. He gently touched my hand and I knew immediately it was the Holy Spirit. Our hearts met and united in a euphoric medley.

The first words spoken, were not spoken at all. With mental telepathy he said, "It is time to review your life Lydia."

Without saying a word, I agreed as he turned to the book with my initials and birth date. Taking the book from the shelf, he opened it to the first page.

Without moving, I was instantly placed in a hospital room where the hustle and bustle of the delivery room was in full swing. The baby was just being birthed and the doctor was cleaning her airways with a small syringe.

"AWWWHHH, how cute," I said, looking at the adorable little face. I knew it had to be me because it was my mother on the delivery table and my father was standing beside her holding her hand. My mom and dad were so excited. After a little crying from the infant, the delivering doctor laid the precious bundle on my mother's chest while he began removing the afterbirth.

I could feel my mother's and father's excitement. I was feeling their feelings. It made me so happy. Now I knew the moment that I came into the world, they were overjoyed. During my whole life with them, I never knew that. I always wondered. By the time I was old enough to understand anything, their marriage had depleted into a troubled union. This moment of joy between the two would now be cherished in my memory forever.

The Holy Spirit turned a few pages. I was instantly taken to a time when I was a toddler. I was playing in the yard. We were all dressed in Easter outfits.

I said, "Hey, I remember those outfits!" I have pictures of us in them. I was running around playing and my older sister was sitting on the swing. She must have been stuck with the task of watching me, I thought. In the background I heard arguing from the house. It sounded like mom and dad. Shortly, my dad walked out and had a bag in his hand. He was upset and heading down the sidewalk to the car. He immediately stopped, dropped his suitcase and walked over in the yard to pick me up.

"I love you," he said, I felt he wanted to cry. I am feeling his heart breaking as if it were my own. He walked over with me in his arms to the swing. My sister stood up and he hugged her. He repeated, "I love you, sweetheart," to her as well. I knew it was bad, because my sister burst into tears. The pain was awful. I was feeling his pain, her pain, my pain; I even felt my mother's pain coming from the house.

"I have to go," he said as he sat me down and headed for his suitcase. He quickly walked down the sidewalk and got into his car and left.

"So that's how it happened," I said, not only to the Holy Spirit, but to myself as well.

The Holy Spirit just looked at me and nodded yes. He then turned a few more pages.

We were in my dad's truck and he was pulling up in front of the house I grew up in. He stopped the truck and got out on his side. "Come on, honey. Wake up. You're home."

I rubbed my eyes and said, "Please don't leave me, daddy."

"I know, baby. I will see you next week. We go through this every time. No crying, ok?" He knew I was going to cry, because every time he left me, I would hang on for dear life not wanting him to leave me.

"So, this is where my abandonment issues began." I started thinking through the dilemma. The emotions were complex. I do remember every time I left on Fridays to spend the weekend with my dad, I would cry as I left, not wanting to leave mom. Then, when he brought me back, I would cry because I didn't want to leave him. I could not be settled emotionally because, at all times, I felt part of me was empty, missing the parent I was not with at the time. Those emotions held fast until my dad passed away when I was the age of nine.

With that, the Holy Spirit turned more pages in the book. He stopped. It was the day of my father's funeral. I was screaming, lying on my dad's coffin. My mother was trying to pull me off of his casket, but I held tight and could not be consoled.

"I don't want to leave him here," I cried.

As I watched the scene, I realized tears were streaming

down my face. I was feeling the emotions of the day. The father I loved with all of my heart would no longer be a presence in my life. It was a devastating event.

The Holy Spirit came to me and put his arms around me. He held me until he felt it was time to continue.

He turned the pages in the book again. He stopped and looked at me with concern.

We were in the house I grew up in. My stepfather was throwing things during one of his many temper tantrums. He grabbed his belt and started hitting my sister with it. I just stood there quivering in fear. I knew myself, as did the scared little girl, that she would not escape his wrath, that she was next. Once he felt he had beaten my sister enough, he turned to me, and began beating me. My mother tried to stop him, but he began hitting her with his fist as well. Once he shoved her out of the way, he began on me again. As an onlooker, I was enraged and wanted to jump in and stop it. I was feeling the pain he was inflicting on me with every welt he inflicted on my skin. The Holy Spirit laid his hand on me to calm me. My heart was pounding hard and I felt I was spinning out of control watching this. I felt the first shameful emotion that would envelope me again and again during this journey. I hate him! I hate him! I hate him! A feeling of rage overpowered my emotions with this act of cruelty.

The Holy Spirit turned the pages again.

I was out in the backyard playing when my stepfather yelled for me to come over to help him. I was twelve years old. I remember the day clearly. He had a ladder propped up against the house.

He said, "I need you to come over here and help me." We all knew to obey or he would throw one of his many fits.

I walked over and he directed me to climb the ladder onto the roof of the house. I said, "I'm too scared to go up there. I'm afraid I'll fall."

"Shut up, and do as I say."

I climbed up on the roof, trembling with fear. He made me walk to the edge of the roof and stand there holding the antenna, while he attached brackets to hold it in place. I stood there watching him and, as I watched him, I saw he was on the very edge of the roof. I watched myself as the child being able to hear every thought going on in that small child's brain. I remembered those thoughts all too well. "I could push him now and he would fall." I let go of the antenna with one hand and held it in midair to push him. As I was about to do it; something inside gave me pause, "What if he doesn't die. Then, he will kill me." I pulled my hand back and held on to the antenna until my knuckles were white.

I looked over at the Holy Spirit and mouthed the words, "I'm sorry. I felt so much shame, so much hate, that I could contemplate murder. The remorse I had at that moment was gut wrenching. How had I let a man drive me to think those thoughts? In the next moment, I knew how. Since my own father's passing, he had taken much pleasure in beating my sister and me. My dad was no longer around to protect us, and he reminded us of that often.

"Call your daddy now," he said one day while taking the belt and beating my sister. I sat on the couch knowing I would be next. I began screaming like he had already beaten me. My mother had already been beaten into submission. What started it in the first place was my sister trying to pull him off of my mother.

"I don't know if I can do this anymore," I said to the Holy Spirit.

He said, "Enough for now.

9

EMOTIONAL MEMORIES

Back in the library, I looked at the Holy Spirit and had to ask why God would allow these things to happen to a child? He took my hand and guided me to a small seating area.

"God suffers too, when children are hurt. I know you cannot see this now, but your suffering has helped make you the person you are, thus, this gift, the unveiling of heaven to you."

"I am here because of the pain I endured?"

"No," he replies, "in spite of the pain. God loves you very much. You have felt abandoned many times, but he has never left you. God the Trinity, and your Guardian Angel (Specter) has been by your side every moment."

"I'm sure you are right. It's just that I didn't feel him during those times. Why didn't he let my stepfather die instead of my dad?"

"Each soul has taken on a life they have chosen for themselves or was chosen for them and, with each life and choice, there is an outcome, a lesson that person has selected to learn. Your father chose a life that ended at the age of 42. It hurt him to leave you, but he has kept watch over you since his departure. You find it easy to blame God for every bad thing that happens, yet, he too is saddened by the many unnecessary decisions that cause hurt or pain. He allows free choice. He sees poor choices, but he loves everyone unconditionally. What you fail to see is that he is always there to pick you up if you turn to him. He will see you through it. Blame is not the answer here, Lydia. When you decided on this life, you, too, made a choice for the experience and growth you will gain, even if it causes another pain. Things are not as black and white as we'd like to believe them to be. It is not for you to know the purpose behind certain events. Besides, God can use bad situations to bring about greater good. You must learn to trust him."

Feeling ashamed again, I answer, "You're right! I must admit, I do fall short in the *trust him* department. He must be disappointed in me."

"God loves you, Lydia. He knows your heart inside and out. He knows your love for him is deeper than the pain you have endured."

"I am ready to continue," I announced.

With that, he turned the pages of the book held firmly in his hands.

We return in a flash to my past. I am in my childhood bedroom upstairs listening to music on the radio. I hear my mother yelling for me to come down to set up for lunch. I immediately panic. I know this day!

Elvis Presley is on the radio. I want to hear this song that I loved, but I never delay when asked to do something for fear my stepfather would get involved. I passed through the living room where my stepfather and my younger siblings were sitting. They were watching a baseball game on TV. I went to the dining room to set up. The stereo was already on, so I changed the dial to the station where Elvis was playing. I started singing with the song and began placing the plates, glasses, and silverware on the table. I watched myself, the 15 year old, complete the set up, and my heart began to pound! I knew exactly what happens next. The Holy Spirit embraces me as we watch.

"Who the hell changed that channel?" he yelled, entering the room.

"I did," I said. "You were watching baseball. I didn't think you would mind. I thought mom had it on."

"Is that your stereo? How many times have I told you not to touch it?" he yelled.

Defending my actions, only seemed to make him madder. Before I knew it, he was coming around the table to smack me across my face. I had an automatic impulse to duck. Bad move! He began chasing me around the table, and picked up a glass and threw it at me as hard as he could. The glass shattered, cutting the back of my elbow. The shattered glass made cuts all over my hands too. You would have thought he cut a main artery from the amount of blood that gushed from my arm. For the first time, I not only feared his rage, but I feared for my life. I ran to the bathroom, slammed the door shut, and locked it. I just stood there, crying. I didn't know how to stop the bleeding. Blood was everywhere. Puddles were on the floor and in the sink.

My mother, who had not been in the room, didn't know what had happened, but she heard me crying. She came to the bathroom door and asked, "What's wrong?"

"I'm hurt," I yelled.

"Open the door so I can see," she said.

I didn't want to for fear he would get in, but I opened it out of sheer panic. When she walked in, she gasped at the sight of all of the blood. I slammed the door behind her, and locked it.

"Oh my God!" she yelled. "What happened?"

"He cut me!"

He heard us in the bathroom and told us to let him in.

"You cut her!" she yelled at him.

"Let me in to see what happened," he said with fake sincerity.

Mom fell for it and opened the door. "We need to get her to the hospital, she needs stitches," she said in a panic.

He walked in. I saw immediately, as he looked at the blood everywhere, that he was about to go off again. He began slapping mom for helping me.

"She deserves it!" he yelled. "Now shut up," he said while looking at me with disgust. "I didn't do half of what I wanted to do to you. Now clean this effing (you know the word) mess up."

He walked out the door. I jumped up and slammed the door behind him. I didn't want him to hit me, or my mom, again. Mom's face was red from the beating and her hand was beginning to swell. I just sat down on the toilet and began low sobbing.

"I can't do this anymore, Mom."

"I know honey, neither can I." With that, she slipped out of the room and came back with a handful of money and a packed bag for me. She said, "Go to the hospital, get stitches, then go to Liddy's house when you leave the hospital. Tell her I will get in touch with her."

"I'm scared," I said.

"I know, honey, but I would not get in the car with him as mad as he is."

I knew that to be the truth. He drove like a mad man when he was angry. So, I took the overnight bag and left with a towel wrapped around my arm to catch the blood.

I began the long 15 mile walk to town. I had gotten about five miles when a friend of mine and her mother saw me. They pulled over to offer me a ride. The mother was frantic with all of the blood. She immediately took me to the hospital, where I was stitched and released. The hospital wanted to know how it had happened. I told them my stepfather did it. They had not listened intently because they ended up reporting my father as the one who did it. Checking the records, they found my father was deceased.

Because, they thought I was lying about it. I was sent home without a police report.

With that thought, I found myself back in the Library. The Holy Spirit was still holding me. His essence had a calming effect on me.

"You have endured a lot," he said in a comforting tone.

"I have become tough through the years, but it remains difficult for me to see a child suffering abuse like that. Not only that, but the way my family suffered. I remember him coming home one day, deciding he didn't like what my mother had prepared for dinner, and throwing it through the window, glass and all. Or the time he came home to find us not watching his favorite TV show. He threw the iron through the TV, causing the TV to burst into flames. It was not just me who was mistreated; it was the whole family. The reviews, I assume, are just incidents pertaining to me, but it was just as painful to watch him attack my family members. He was a monster. As you know, the hardest thing for me was to stand over his casket and say; I forgive you."

The Holy Spirit said, "You forgave him long before that day. Don't you remember going to see him when he was in the hospital after the car accident? If forgiveness hadn't filled your heart, you would have never gone. In the end, this life is about love. It is easy to love those who love you. It is harder to love those who do not know how to love, or those hard to love."

"Was my stepfather damaged?" I asked, feeling as though I already knew the answer.

He answered, "His father was a sick man. He ruled the same way. Your stepfather's father ended up killing himself. He learned parenting from a man who was just as cruel. He lived the same anger as a child that he imposed on you as an adult. They both used anger to invoke fear. He found by producing this same result he got his way.

I asked, "Why, then, did I not do the same thing to my daughter? If anything, I wanted to do the exact opposite. I probably over-loved her."

He smiled. "Over-loving? No, I don't think you did that. You have been by your daughter's side through everything. She knows you love her, and she is confident she can depend on you."

"I hope so," I responded while pondering our relationship.

He brings me back to our mission by asking, "Are you ready to continue?"

Not quite certain of my emotional state, I responded, "As long as you are with me."

10

TOMATO SOUP

As the next page turned, I let myself be drawn into the mechanics of it. There was no vehicle that was propelling me forward, nor did I ever feel unsteady. I felt as though I was moving, then again, I felt like I moved nowhere. When all became clear, I was in another time in my life. Trying to make sense of it was impossible. It defied gravity, motion, and modern science.

In this new vision, I was seventeen years old. I was in the apartment I had obtained after I left home, years after the cutting. It was a small place. Each room was no larger than a 10 ft. by 10 ft. The bedroom was only large enough for a twin bed and a dresser. The kitchen was a little corner area at the end of my living room. It was the "open concept" before open concept was popular. It could not be called an efficiency, because the bedroom was separate. But, it suited my needs entirely. I sat there curled on my couch doing my homework.

After I left home the day he cut me, I didn't return. My mom sent me a check every month for $220.00. These checks were from the social security office. Mom began receiving them after my dad's death for child support. It was just enough to get me by. I rented a fully furnished apartment with utilities for $200.00 a month. That left $5.00 weekly for groceries.

My daily schedule consisted of going to school for half a day, then to work at a local burger joint from twelve to five. It was great, because there was time for homework even though I worked five or six days a week. I never missed a day of school for fear the school would know I was living alone before my eighteenth birthday.

The Holy Spirit said to me, "This is where you proved you were strong. You alone took care of your needs. You supported yourself with very little, and managed to make it. God was especially attentive to you in those years. He knew you were alone and he sometimes felt your uncertainty."

I responded, "You know, I should have been afraid being all alone at such a young age of 15, but without the beatings and anger all around me, I found such peace being alone. I could walk into my home and no one would hurt me. It felt good!"

"I know," he said. "You made peace with your

situation by not having the threat of bodily harm. This next memory will show more struggle. My heart ached for you." He looked at me with warmth and love and it spilled over like liquid gold into my heart. "I wanted to show myself to you, to pick you up and hold you," he said.

He turned the page and I was in my apartment again. I was sitting at the window looking out, as it had been snowing. I remember that day, I thought. It had snowed so much, I couldn't get out to go to work. In fact, work was closed due to weather. I had been out of money for a few days, and out of food. I should have already picked up my paycheck, but the weather prevented it. I had forty-two cents to my name. I watched myself as a teenager walk to the kitchen to look for food. There was absolutely nothing left to eat. It was 6:00 p.m. and I hadn't eaten anything that day. I decided to take the forty-two cents to the Seven-Eleven, a block down the street, hoping to find something to buy that would sustain me until the roads were clear tomorrow. Everywhere I looked down the street, there was no movement. Cars were snow covered and no one had begun the shoveling that would indicate life's movements again.

I put on my boots and wrapped up snug for warmth. I put my gloves on and walked out of the apartment. It was no longer snowing, but the snow was already deep, almost knee high. The wind was whipping, too.

I told the Holy Spirit, "It was just beginning to get dark so, as I recall, the decision was a last minute one to go."

He nodded acknowledgement of my statement and continued to watch the younger me taking one step at a time in the deep snow. When I got to the road, I could walk in the tire marks, although there were very few.

I arrived at the store and walked up and down the aisles, looking for the best buy for my forty- two cents. After much deliberation, I decided on a can of tomato soup and a bottle of Pepsi. Fingers still cold from the frigid weather, I counted out the few cents I had to pay for the two items. I purchased both and left the store. As I walked out of the store, the wind hit me square in the face. The snow was blowing, and stepping into the deep snow was a great challenge. I slowly made each deep step until reaching the end of the Seven-Eleven parking lot. My plan was to cross to the other side of the street. As I took the first step from the snow to the road, I lost my balance. The surface was compacted with snow that had turned hard as ice. I went down. Hard! My arms were flailing trying to catch myself. Crash! The bottle of Pepsi broke into pieces. The realization of the broken bottle hit me like a ton of bricks. The last few cents I had to my name may just as easily have been thrown in the trash for what just happened. I lay there on the ground, crying. Not just a whimper, but a give up sob that shook my whole body.

It couldn't have been written with more sadness in a movie, I thought, as I watched myself crying. My Guardian Angel appeared rubbing my back to comfort me as I lay in the snow crying. My emotions reached new heights seeing his presence. At the time, I thought I was alone that day. I wish I could have felt him then, I thought as I watched the scene play out.

Up until this point, I had not really taken a good look at my Guardian Angel. He had said I could call him Specter. He had the kindest face and eyes. I thought, as I watched him, that he had a fatherly look. I'm not sure what I mean by that, just that he seemed to hover as my protector like any good father would do. He had a firm build to imply that he could handle himself if he had to go into battle. Yet, there was this softness, the way he was seeing to my needs in those distressed moments. I felt an intimate knowledge of him, too, as if he were a very close loved one, similar to a family member. I knew I had felt this earlier. And again at this moment, I felt he was a warm place for my heart to be.

I watched myself get up and make my way back to the house. My Guardian Angel walked by my side, holding my elbow as if he were assisting me. I retraced my steps in the deep snow back to my warm apartment and went inside.

Once there, I trashed the broken Pepsi bottle, opened the soup to cook on the stovetop, and pour myself a glass of water. My nourishment was limited to liquids that night, as I didn't have a single piece of bread or cracker to put in my soup. I recall how good it tasted though. The tomato soup was thick and warm on my dry tongue. It rolled down my throat adding the warmth that my cold body needed. I was so hungry. I wonder if that is why I love tomato soup so much?

I have always known lack it seems; lack of food, lack of money, and lack of love. When I was a little girl, my stepfather lost his job. We had nothing in the house but flour. My mother used that flour to make pancakes and gravy for us. I was very hungry then too, and it tasted so good. Food was never a primary focus for any of us as kids. With six kids to feed, you always received a small portion for each serving. Of course, I didn't mind. As I think back, I was never really that hungry when I was young. I would rather go to my room, or go out to play than eat. My mother used to have to call me in at night. I would stay outside all day, never wanting to come in. I built an Indian tipi to hang out in. Poochie and I would stay in there all day.

The Holy Spirit watched me as my mind went back to thinking about those precious moments. Knowing my thoughts, he smiled at me. We embraced, and he turned another page.

11

FOR BETTER OR FOR WORSE

The page turned and I saw myself seated in a small restaurant. It was a hangout for many young adults. Cars would cruise through the lot, or you could park, come in, and hang out. I saw I was with my cousin, Dina, sitting at a booth when he walked in. Brad was tall, dark, and handsome. Just to die for. Anyway, he looked my way, and I gave him a quick smile before turning my head. I looked at Dina and shot an eyebrow up to let her know I was interested. We had that girl code between us. When guys flirt, we look to each other for encouragement and validation. In this case, I was definitely interested. I hadn't seen him around for a while. My initial thought was that he must have been involved with someone, not to be in the circuit lately. He pulled up in a nice sports car, a Camaro. It was a sign he had a good job.

Ordering a coke with ice, he walked over to my booth, and asked if he could join us.

"Sure," I said, a little shocked at his direct approach.

"So, what have you girls been up to?" he asked,

looking straight at me.

"Not much, just hanging out," we both said at the same time.

"Would the two of you like to cruise for a while?" he asked.

I looked to Dina for guidance and she said, "Sure, why not?"

He motions the waitress over for our bill, pays it, and we get up to leave with him. I know what you're thinking, but no, he wasn't a stranger. We lived in a small town where everyone knows everyone else. Brad and I had known each other all of our lives. We went to school together, we saw each other at the pool during summer vacations, and we typically saw each other at just about every event in town. This, however, is the first time we decided to cruise together. To my delight, he had grown up so much; he looked much older than I remembered him. I guess we aren't kids anymore, I thought.

We rode for hours before ending up in the parking lot hang out, where a bunch of other friends had gathered. We had a great time, laughing and talking about everything and nothing. I enjoyed talking about school and old friends. Many of us had not seen Brad since he had been away in the service. He informed us he was stationed in Arkansas, that is why he hadn't been around.

We spent hours at the parking lot catching up. The evening soon turned into night; too soon it was time to go home. We dropped Dina off at her car, and then he drove me to my apartment. During that night, I had listened intently while he told of his many adventures around the world as an Air Force loadmaster with the 314 Tactical Airlift Wing, under the control of the Military Airlift Command (MAC). In layman's terms, he controlled weight distributions on the plane, by making sure planes did not exceed load capacity. He was proud of his position on the crews, along with the pilots, navigators and flight engineers, that flew the C130 Hercules, and he really loved the Air Force.

After we dropped off Dina, we sat in his car and talked for hours. He was not involved with anyone, nor was I. He would be in town for two more weeks, so we made plans to go out again. He walked me to the door and gave me a gentle kiss on the lips. It was a very good night.

I called Dina the next day and we giggled like little girls. I was so excited to have someone new to crush on. We had so much in common, I told her during our girl session. He was the quiet type, and not a player at all. He preferred to be in a committed relationship, which suited me just fine. I told Dina that we had plans for the next two weeks while he was in town.

Those two weeks went by with the blink of an eye. Before long, he was packed and leaving to go back to the Air Force Base in Little Rock, Arkansas. It was two glorious weeks of nonstop quality time together. When he left, I thought I would be lost forever. We wrote letters constantly. First, just telling each other about our days, then moving more into the "I miss you" phase. He called every couple of weeks. Before I knew it, six months had passed, and the holidays had arrived.

He told me he had received leave and he would be coming home for the holidays. I was so excited to receive the news. This time, he took me to meet his parents, where we spent the holidays visiting his relatives. I felt I had met my soul-mate in him. Our long letters and talks on the phone, gave us ample time to become better acquainted on a deeper level. Being in his arms was like home for me, so when the words of love were spoken during that holiday, it felt right. When he left, I felt empty. Dina would try to get me to go out, but I preferred writing him and waiting on his calls. He, too, hated our separation.

He surprised me on Valentine's Day by showing up

unannounced. When I opened the door to my apartment, I was shocked. There he stood in my doorway. I ran into his arms and, like a child, jumped up on him, screaming. We laughed so hard at my reaction.

He said, "Grab your coat."

"Why, where are we going?"s

"It's a surprise," he said, grinning from ear to ear.

We drove to an overlook on the mountain. It was dark, and all you could see were the lights of the city below. He talked about his feelings for me, and how he couldn't go on without me. It was pretty mushy for him. I watched myself gushing like a child. I looked at the Holy Spirit who was smiling with delight.

"The bottom line is, I love you," Brad says as he pulls out a box. Inside the box was a diamond in a tiffany six prong setting, just like I had always wanted. He had rigged a light inside the box to illuminate the stone in the dark. It was so romantic.

I couldn't believe this whole thing. Him, me, getting married?! All of my dreams were coming true! This was an answer to my prayers, for sure. This wonderful man asking for my hand in marriage was making me delirious. We sat for hours that night making plans. I looked at the man that I would soon call my husband, and I saw love in his eyes. I saw hands that would hold mine forever, and arms that would keep me warm from the cold and cradle our children.

We set plans in motion. He was only home for a couple of days. He moved in that night and we set about the task of consolidating our lives. We decided I didn't need my car because he had two, so we placed an ad to sell mine. We called my landlord and gave a month's notice. We met with the minister to lock in a date. March 4th would be our day! It was all set, and ready to go.

He would only have a few days leave for our wedding. We planned to marry here at home. After that, I would move to Arkansas to be with him. We made as many arrangements as possible in those few days together, then, he left. I began packing and assembling my life in preparation for the move.

After Brad left, I went about getting ready for my part of the wedding. I shopped for dresses and flowers. Every day was filled with completing tasks that would inevitably culminate in my new life.

I had been out all day a few Saturdays later. When I

finally arrived home that day, I felt exhausted. I spent the day with Dina, talking about my wedding plans and shopping for my gown. Of course, she was in the wedding. When I returned home to my apartment that afternoon around 3:00 p.m., I went in to lay down for a bit. I grabbed the mail on the way through the door. Sitting on top was a beautiful card from Brad. He said he was leaving for one of his trips and wouldn't be able to talk to me for a few days. He wrote on the card that every minute without me was torture. He couldn't wait until he was home from the trip and we could get married. He signed it, "I love you now, forever, and through eternity."

How sweet, I thought as I held the card to my chest and dropped off to sleep.

I was startled awake by the door bell ringing. My heart was pounding from the abrupt wake up. I got off the bed and walked to the front door. I opened it to see Susie, Brad's cousin. She saw me, and from my sleepy eyes she assumed I had been crying.

She said, "You've heard?"

"Heard what?" I asked, confused.

"About the plane crash Brad was in last night, he didn't make it" she blurted out.

I screamed, "What!?!"

"It couldn't be. I just got a card from him today. Someone has gotten the wrong information," I said, still fighting the panic that wanted to grab me.

She pulled me to the couch and sat me down. "No. The Air Force sent a military officer to his mother's house a couple of hours ago. His parents tried to call you."

"I have been out all day," I said, my voice beginning to crack. I looked over at the answering machine and saw the light was blinking.

"NNNNNNNNNNNNOOOOOOOOOOOOOOOO OOOOOOO!!!!" I cried. "It can't be true. Not Brad. Please not Brad." Then, I lost all control. I cried without restraint. Susie was unable to console me.

After she made calls to Dina and my family, she left to go back to Brad's mother's house. I couldn't go. I wanted to be alone, alone with my devastation, my anger, and my shock. I went to my room and I didn't come out for days. I was blindly led through the funeral. I couldn't stand to look at his family. Seeing his father's face whose resemblance was remarkable to Brad's, tortured me.

I went through the next month in a daze. I tried as I

could to get back to my life but, since his death, I couldn't get going again. I didn't want to eat. I lost at least 15 lbs. during that month. What made matters worse was getting the flu after not eating enough. I was so weak, I was bedridden. Family and friends were saying it was depression and I had to pull myself together, but when the nausea set in, I knew it had to be the flu.

I went to the doctor and he confirmed I had a bug. He ran some tests and said he would call me in a few days with the results. Right now, I was to let it run its course. If the tests came back telling him something different, he would contact me. His orders were to go home, eat, and get some rest.

Two days later, the doctor's office called. He said "Lydia, you do not have the flu. You're pregnant."

"What?!" I exclaimed.

"You are definitely pregnant. We did the blood work and you are about eight weeks along."

Thinking back, yes that would be right, I thought to myself. "Thank you for the call," I said to the doctor trying to cover the panic in my voice.

"Well," he said. "Let me know if you need something

for the nausea. You will need to set up a follow-up appointment so that we can get you on prenatal vitamins."

"Thank you, doctor. I will call back later," I said, still shocked at what he was really saying to me.

I sat down, letting it all sink in. Clutching my stomach, I cried yet again. This time it was tears of joy. Brad had given me a gift to remember him always. What was it he said?

"I love you now, forever and through eternity."

Our baby was proof of that love. I looked at the Holy Spirit who had relived this time with me, and he repeated the word to me, ETERNITY. Then he turned the page.

12

DEFINE SIN

"Let's take a break," the Holy Spirit said to me. Reliving that experience was pretty traumatic for you.

"Yes," I said still feeling the misery.

We stood up from the couch and moved toward two French doors. Opening the doors, we walked out onto a beautiful stone patio. Along its edges, were flowers that appeared to be organized as part of some grand design. Every flower was placed methodically. I took a deep breath and inhaled the sweet aroma.

Suddenly, Poochie emerged from the field trotting across the grass at a high rate of speed. She jumped over the flowers and playfully circled me several times. I laughed and began running, chasing her. We romped until I was spent and fell to the grass. Even the grass had a fragrance to it, you know, that freshly cut scent. She was jumping on me and pushing me with her cold nose. I rough housed with her a bit. As I stood up, I saw the Holy Spirit walking towards me, or was he floating? I can never tell. I watched as he narrowed the gap between us.

Without warning his body began transforming into Jesus. I froze and just paused there, watching His Grace make his way to me, smiling as he approached.

"You've had an intense morning. How are you doing with all of this?" He asked this while taking my hand and pulling me back down to the ground to sit.

"This sure does bring back a lot of grief, it has been quite the review," I said, thinking about what I witnessed. "Are you disappointed in me?"

He asked, "For what?"

I knew he knew, but he was making me say it. "You know, child out of wedlock, sex without marriage. Yadah, Yadah."

He laughed. "Yadah, Yadah?"

"Well, I'm nervous talking to you about this. I say stupid things when I'm nervous," I said, still feeling uncomfortable about this conversation.

His reply to my silly response was, "Let us recall Paul's words to the people of Corinth when he reminded them of what's important: now these three remain: faith, hope and love, but the greatest of these is love. Was there love between you and Brad? I am not talking about lust. I am talking about capital L-O-V-E."

I answered an emphatic, "Yes!"

He asks again, "Were you getting married? Was your heart committed in love for him?"

I answered again, "Yes."

"Then I see nothing that stands between you and the spirit of our Father's law. When you chose to follow me, I did not need a contract to know your love. I felt it. You showed it. We loved one another. If you know in your heart that you were committed to Brad, are you not then displaying love in accordance to my will?" The marriage vows, as you traditionally know them, are a man-made public expression of your commitment to one another. Have you read of any requirement for Adam and Eve to have a formal ceremony? No. It was not necessary. My law that you love one another, heart and soul, is sufficient. I knew your heart, so I knew your soul was in line with the will of God."

I asked, "Does that mean I am guilty of knowing too little of your word and I lack full understanding? Is that what you are trying to tell me?"

He said, "Let love rather than the law, be your guide.

Do all things in love. Your daughter was conceived in love, Lydia. Never be ashamed of that."

"Thank you so much for blessing my relationship with Brad. It means so much to me," I said.

"You are the blessing," he says adding a hug. Looking toward the two French doors, he said, "now go, someone wants to talk with you."

Turning, I see Brad standing in front of the doors I had come out of. I kissed Jesus before running to join Brad.

13

'TIL DEATH DO US PART

Being back in the arms of the man I had always loved and lost, was the most exhilarating, momentous, feeling I had ever experienced. He was so handsome. I believed he was even more handsome than in life. I looked at those gorgeous dark eyes, the ones that were a mirror image to my daughter's eyes. They melted me and made my heart swell.

"Death suits you," I said with humor behind the words. It's strange that I can now find humor in death. Before, the word death mangled my heart into shreds as I thought of it.

"You are so beautiful, even more so," he says holding my face in his hands. "Let's take a walk. I have something to share with you."

Taking my hand we began strolling through a garden. We walked down a pebbled path, lined with beautiful trees and flowers. The beauty is beyond description, with the radiance of the sun's light showering the landscape. The rays were kissing each flowered petal with warmth and love, everything was so alive. I am not familiar with flower names, but I recognized the roses and carnations. They were always my favorites. Multitudes of brilliantly colored flowers were everywhere. Here they were in many colors, colors I had never even seen before. Even baby's breath grew among the roses. The air I inhaled seemed to electrify my senses. It made me see more. I saw the tiniest details of events taking place. As I looked at each flower, I was pulled by the next to stand in awe again. None were more pleasing than the other. For the first time, I noticed the dirt had life; I could clearly see a brown sparkle to it. If I didn't know better, I would think it was glittered dirt. I was in awe of every sight before me.

"You know," Brad said, interrupting my thoughts. "I have never left you. It was difficult for me to see you in so much pain when I died. I was not there to witness it at first. I went through the normal processing here. Then I went through review, like you are doing now. That's when I saw you and all you were going through. It broke my heart. I pleaded to go back to you."

"I am learning the ways of death," I said, understanding what he was telling me. "Brad, even though you died, I still remained committed to you. It was as if our vows had been taken. It was for better or for worse with me, and I just happened to get the **worse** when you died. I never stopped loving you and wanting to be your wife. Even death could not separate me from you. No one could replace what we had. I will go to my grave with you in my heart. Do you know about your child, Brad?"

"Oh, yes," he said gathering me in his arms. "She's so beautiful!"

"She looks like you, you know. That's why you think she's so beautiful," I said punching him in the ribs playfully. "I named her Christi, after Christ. I couldn't figure out how to name her after you. Had the two famous actors Brad Pitt and Angelina Jolie gotten together earlier, I could have used their name Bradgelina," I said trying to be playful with him.

"The name, Christi, is perfect. She is perfect," he says. "I have watched over her and been with her every minute. I am so proud of what she has become. She has the purest heart," he gushes. "And she is mine," he exclaimed with pride.

"Yes, she is, Brad. You left me the most wonderful, cherished gift. Our child is a beautiful blessing to my life, and so are you, I say with the purest sincerity."

"I want to see her," he said. "Let's go together to

check on her."

I looked at him surprised with such a request. A request, I admit, I had no answer for. I turned around to see if Jesus was still around to ask. He came out of nowhere walking across the lawn to us.

Brad took the initiative to ask as Jesus approached. "May we check on Christi? I know she must be devastated over her mother's illness."

Jesus replied, "It will be the same as always Brad, you can only watch. She will not be able to see you. You will not be able to help her as a human is able to. Are you satisfied with that limited access?"

Brad replied, "I just need to be there for her, and for her to know, one day, that I was always with her. So, yes, that is acceptable."

Jesus looked at me, "What about you? This may alter your decision to stay here or to return. Are you ok with that?"

I responded after searching Brad's loving eyes for an answer. I have the choice of staying here with Brad, and so many I love, or go back to a life that I have been so unhappy with. After Brad's death, the only joy in my life was my daughter. I looked at Jesus and asked, "Will I be able to come back here after we check on her?"

Jesus said, "It is always your choice to stay or go. This experience will benefit you either way. If you choose to stay here," he turns and gestures his hands toward the house, "your lessons will continue. If you choose to return to life on earth, you will return with a new message about life and its purpose. Either way, it is a choice only you can make."

I responded with a troubled heart, "But don't you understand, I want Brad **and** Christi. I want mom, dad, Chad, and Poochie too! Why do I have to choose one or the other? No matter what I choose, I will be without one of them."

"This is true," Jesus replied. "But once you have completed your lessons here, life will not be so hard. You will fully understand your purpose and come to terms with Brad's purpose. You will see what lies in store for all of your family members so much clearer than before. You will find peace and happiness for their journeys, and even support them. You will be together again. Knowing that will give you the peace and understanding you need to be content, if that is the path you choose."

With that, the decision was made for Brad and I to go to Christi.

14

IN MY IMAGE

Jesus went into light form and began circling Brad and I in his light. As the light faded, we were standing in a hospital room. My body was lying in a small hospital bed, still comatose. Machines were mechanically breathing for my lifeless body. The unit was making a clicking sound for each breath it made on my behalf.

I watched Brad walk around the bed. He leaned down and kissed my immobile body on the cheek. I stood there watching, and looked at him with all of his youth and good looks, and wondered why he would have the urge to do that to a 50 some year old woman. He looked at me and said, "I have been with you every day since I left. I watched you age to your 50's and I loved you every minute of every day. He picked up my lifeless pale hand, held it in his, and kissed it."

I didn't know what to say. I felt embarrassed at my insignificant thought of vanity. He walked back over to me, put his arms around me, and held me.

He said, "You were and are everything to me, Lydia. I

am so glad you kept me in your heart. Although you haven't seen me for all of these years, I have been with you constantly. Time passes differently here. For me, it was like yesterday that I left you in death. For you, it has been almost 30 years."

I noticed a subtle movement from the far corner of the room. To my surprise, I saw Specter, my Guardian Angel. At intervals, Specter would hover over my body. He would rub my forehead to soothe me. My body, lying there, gave no response to his touch, but I could feel his touch as I stood near the bed. I felt supported by him. At the mere thought of my comfort, and without words, Specter looked at me and smiled. The warmth that ran between us was reassuring.

Just as Brad released me from a tender hold, Christi walked in. Brad turned immediately and stood, mesmerized, watching his daughter. She laid her purse on the chair and walked over to where my immobile body laid. She looked very upset as she grabbed my limp hand.

"Mom, I just spoke to the doctor, he said it's all up to you now. Please fight!"

My sister, Carly, walked in and grabbed Christi, hugging her. "It'll be ok, Christi. Your mom's a fighter.

Have you talked to the doctor yet?"

Christi answered, "Yes. He said she had an aneurism. They will not know the damage until she wakes up, if she wakes up. He told me they performed a surgery on her called coil embolization. During the procedure, a small tube was inserted into the affected artery and positioned near the aneurysm. They moved tiny metal coils through the tube into the aneurysm, relieving pressure making it less likely to rupture. It's up to her now to recover." Christi begins to cry. "Just repeating what he said sends me into a panic," Christi continues through her tears, "I can't believe this. She seemed so healthy."

"I know," Carly said. "She didn't complain at all to me. Did she say anything to you about headaches? Anything?"

"Well, before she went to bed last night, she did say she had a headache. We had been laughing at dinner, having a great time, so I thought nothing of it."

During Christi and Carly's exchange, Brad walked over to Christi and laid his hand on her back for comfort. I wanted her to look around at him, but, of course, she couldn't feel his touch. He was looking at his daughter with great affection. Looking at me he says, "She is so sad.

She loves you so much."

"I know," I said, tears beginning to fall down my face. How could I consider leaving her alone? She's my only child."

Brad stood watching Christi and said, "Wow, I feel like I am looking at myself. She looks so much like me."

I said with a smile, "We are all made in God's image, but she was definitely made in your image, too. I thank God every day for giving her to me. Every time she looked at me, I could see your eyes looking back. I have pictures of her smiling. She has your smile, you know. Her smile comforts me. I've always felt like a part of you was always with me."

Carly decided she would stay with me while Christi went home to shower and change. Christi had been there by my side all day and night and needed to freshen up. "Christi, have you eaten anything?" Carly asked.

"No. I did stop and buy a Latte. I really didn't want anything. My nerves are so messed up. I don't think I can eat."

Carly said while grabbing her arm. "Let's take a walk to the cafeteria to get you some real food. There is no telling how long your mom will be like this. You need to keep up your strength."

Christi grabs her purse and they left the room.

I looked at the Holy Specter and asked, "Am I going to be ok? Am I going to come out of this?"

"That's totally up to you. You have the choice to return or to stay in heaven. You will need to decide if your life is finished here. You've been granted an awesome gift. To go to heaven and return to this life is not something that happens every day. You will need to decide by the end of your heavenly journey what you want to do."

"I'm so torn! To leave Christi and my family here on earth, or to leave Brad and the rest of my family in heaven is quite a conundrum."

Brad replied, "We will be ok regardless of your decision. This needs to be for you. Decide what you feel. Not what any of us feel. This is your life experience and lesson."

"I know, but I've been so unhappy on earth and I've found my peace in heaven. It is such an easy decision, that is, until I see Christi. My heart breaks as I look at her. If I leave, she will be without both parents. We have been so close. She tells me everything. I'm her confidant and her sounding board. If I leave, who will do that for her?"

The Holy Specter said, "Leaving Christi alone may distress you, but don't let that single struggle guide your decision to stay or go. Your decision needs to be about you. You need to ask yourself have you finished your life on earth? Have you achieved growth in acquiring the knowledge expected of you?"

"I understand. May I finish my journey before I decide?"

The Holy Specter replied, "Of course."

Brad, the Holy Specter and I, sat there in each other's thoughts waiting for Christi and Carly to return. The rest of the family arrived shortly after them. Brad sat beside Christi at the end of my bed, watching and listening as Christi and the family began recalling life events about me. The three of us laughed at some of the stories they told. Some of the stories were a little embarrassing for me, but Brad was always there to put his arms around me. He said, "I would love to have been there." It was such a special moment for me, to hear my family remembering me in love.

Suddenly, the light swirl appeared again. In an instant,

Brad and I were back in the garden. Jesus was there, waiting, and asked me, "Did that help?"

"Yes, it did. Thank you."

"Good. Let's have lunch before we continue your journey." With that, we moved toward the house.

15

FOR GOODNESS SAKE

The three of us walked up to the house to enjoy a festive lunch. The table was spread with great food and drink. We ate while talking about the house, and about how beautiful we found it. Jesus looked at Brad and me. "The two of you," he said, "will be very happy here one day." I looked at Brad and he smiled as he shot his eyebrows up with approval.

Jesus was so personable. I feel like he's my best friend and that Brad and I could talk to him about anything. He was dressed in jeans and casual long sleeved blue shirt. Can you believe that? I suppose I thought it odd for him to be dressed that way. I expected him to be in the long flowing white robe I had always seen him wear in artistic depictions. Brad was dressed in jeans too, only he was wearing a shirt with a dark blue sweater over it. I looked at both men and found both of them quite handsome.

Jesus interrupted my thoughts and said, "Thanks!" Brad said thanks right after that.

We laughed, and continued with small talk.

Something was nagging at me. "Jesus," I asked, "I feel so special that you are here with me. How do you have time to spend with me, when you have all of the heavens to run?"

He replied, nodding his head with understanding, "You continue to think in earthly terms my dear. The nature of a spiritual life permits me to be in more than one place at a time. Ask Brad. I am with him always, at all times."

Brad nodded his head in agreement. "Lydia, it's hard to comprehend, but if you were here under normal circumstances, you would have regained your heavenly memory by now. Heaven is so perfect. My thoughts are your thoughts. You don't need to wonder if you're doing right or wrong, because the Holy Spirit is in you, with you, and around you at all times. Recalling earlier today when we had the question about going to see Christi, we only thought it and Jesus came. There are no worries, no concerns, and no regrets. Everything has to do with living every moment to its fullest. After you return from a life's trip, it's exciting to go before the trinity to speak of your journey in that life." He looked at Jesus and said, "Sorry, I get carried away."

"No problem, son. It makes me happy to hear your

words."

I then asked, "When will I see God?"

Jesus replied, "It's not too long now." With that, he folds his napkin and lays it on the table. Brad and I follow his lead and get up from the table to join him.

"Brad, why don't you take Lydia out for a moment to say goodbye? Lydia, you can then meet me back in the library," Jesus said.

I looked at Brad in dismay. I didn't want to leave the love I had lost so long ago. Brad and I walked out to the back patio and stood holding each other.

"Lydia, I know how this works and for me, it's not so complicated, I still get to see you. You however, can't see me. That's the struggle for you. This will be harder on you than it is on me. What I want to leave you with, is this, our love goes beyond the borders of earth. It even goes beyond the heavens. It's intrinsically in our soul. It is who we are. Go. Live this life and complete your purpose in it, if that is what you choose. Don't let us being apart keep you from making the right decision. I will be with you always, and we will see each other again here. That I can promise. This house, will be our home one day. Forever. This house is our home. It only exists for us. If you are not here, it is not here. This is your ideal heaven, so it will be perfect when you come back to it. Take this gift God has given you and use it to ignite a passionate feel for serving and loving others. Fulfill God's mission, be love for the world to see. Yes, Poochie will be here waiting for you, too," he laughed. "I told you we know each other's thoughts and heart here," he smiled.

With that, Brad and I kissed one last time. We held each other so tight I thought I had become him. As the tears began to fall and with a dramatic goodbye, he was gone.

I stood there taking in all the beauty that filled my soul before I turned to walk back into the library. There, the Holy Spirit was waiting with book in hand. I wondered how the decision was made of who would arrive to meet me, God, Jesus or the Holy Spirit. What I came to understand was that all three were really there, in different forms. He held his hand out and I placed mine in his. As he held my hand, he reached over to the table and turned the page.

Unlike before, these visions were very happy events in my life, each filled with goodness. Life events flashed before me like a movie screen. I saw me paying for the girl's groceries at the grocery store. It was a young girl with a baby. She clearly didn't have enough money to pay for the baby food and formula she needed, so I happily paid for it. I saw me helping my mother with her paper work on her mortgage and assisting her with her Medicare/Medicaid applications. There were visions of me at work, complimenting my employees for a job well done. After my sister, Jeanie, had lost her job, I paid the last car payment for her. The thing is, this viewing also allowed me to feel the emotions of the person I was helping. The gratitude in their hearts and the words they used to describe their feelings after I left. The apparitions of living out the good things I had displayed in my life for others, went on and on. It soon became clear that I did those things with no intent to benefit myself, only to do good for another. I was good only for the sake of goodness.

My heart was warmed. Going through this experience helped me to better understand what the elders mean when they teach us, the best way to forget our pain or sadness is to help others. As I reveled in the glory of giving more love in this lifetime than I actually thought was possible, I felt uplifted. I soared with high emotions. How could I have not seen it? My life had not only been about pain and suffering; it was about the love I passed on to others. Each time I had acted in a place of love, my life would settle into a peaceful stage. From now on, I will look at life through the eyes of love.

I am a better person, seeing all that life had given to me. It served to reinforce my desire to do all things with good intent, to seek a positive result. My heart, it seemed, was always in the right place. Even when things didn't turn out the way I expected. I can recall my family always thinking of me as a controlling person. Having just watched these images, I would have to agree with them. Yet, in each instance, my sole purpose was to solve the problem, not control it. I sought to be a helper, a giver, a confidant, an advice giver. All things were done in the name of goodness and love on my part.

The Holy Spirit gently closed the book. In a flash, the apparitions were gone, and it was just the two of us again. He was smiling broadly. "Well, Lydia, this trip was very pleasant indeed."

With a deep freeing sigh, I replied, "Finally, no torturous memories like before."

"Lydia, you got lost in the shadow of the sadness in your life, while you busied yourself to bring light and joy to others. Your reward in eternity will be great. You have earned many a crown for your love and devotion. You have built a solid foundation to base your remaining life on. If you choose to continue your earthly existence, can you focus on the kind of things we just reviewed instead of living in the shadows of pain?"

"I will certainly try," I said with great commitment in my voice.

Not realizing how long we had reviewed the images, he pointed out it was time for dinner. "Go out, take a breather. Then come back in for dinner when you're ready."

I walked back out on the patio, reminiscing all I had just witnessed. There were so many powerful images in my heart and mind. I found it became overwhelming to realize some good had come from my life. Like so many, I was under the fearful impression I may not go to heaven because I wasn't good enough. As Jesus had said earlier, I had been too tough on myself. Now was the time to listen to my heart. It would help me do the things I needed to do.

I sighed, pulling in a deep breath, before turning to go into the house. I went up the stairs to the main level passing through the library. As I entered the dining area, my eyes could barely contain the surprise that would await me.

16

FAITH IS BELIEVING

There was no long formal dining table as I had expected; instead, there was a small table set for four. I walked up to the table and looked at the place settings. The plates had the appearance of crystal, both sparkling and dazzling. Although the plates were clear, I could see a hint of blue and pink. The glassware held the same hues, with the exception of the tattered wooden goblet, always present. In the center of the table, stood blue and pink flowers. Again, I didn't know the name of these flowers, but, they were beautifully arranged in a short slender vase. An interesting difference to normal cut flowers on most arrangements, these flowers had beautiful roots that were displayed as if arranged in the vase. They were an added green contrast that blended well with the blue and pink. They were so attractively arranged. It appeared to be no vase at all. The flowers commanded my attention as if they were standing on their own.

A commotion coming from the entry way told me I was no longer alone. As I turned to see the guests, to my delight Jesus walked in with the Holy Spirit. They were laughing. Jesus jokingly pushed the Holy Spirit and said "You did not!"

"I tell you, I did," the Holy Spirit said.

They both burst into laughter as Jesus said, "I would love to have witnessed that."

"Well, go ahead," said the Holy Spirit. "Seeing is believing."

They both saw me, and each walked over to give me a kiss on the cheek.

Jesus says, "Sorry we're late. I think this Spirit has had too many spirits before dinner. He is telling me something totally unbelievable." They looked at each other and laughed again as they thought back to their private conversation. Jesus then looked back at me and said, "You look lovely my dear." Jesus held out my arms in approval.

I looked down at myself and saw that I was dressed in a lovely evening dress. This was shocking to me, because I didn't remember changing. It was a straight line, navy blue dress, with a delicate white collar. The sleeves were three quarter length and stopped two inches above my wrist with a white band cuffing the sleeve. "Uh, thank you. The two of you look handsome I must say." They both wore white dress shirts; their ties matched the well creased navy blue slacks. They weren't identically dressed, but pretty darn close. The shades of blues were different, I guess.

The Holy Spirit walked over to the beverage bar and poured four glasses of red wine for us. I thought that strange since there were only three of us. It was then I recalled the fourth place setting at the table. The next moment answered a most important unasked question, as if my thinking made it happen.

Jesus said, "Good evening, Father."

I choked on my drink! I couldn't quit coughing. It was so embarrassing. Jesus touched my arm and I stopped.

"Father?" I said. "THE Father?"

The Holy Spirit, while keeping its form, turned absolutely transparent and began dancing. It was so beautiful. While the Holy Spirit was usually all serious and such, he was now displaying a full range of emotion and color. We stood there watching as the dance of life filled the room. I was giddy, and happy. When he stopped, "Father kissed him on the cheek."

"Thank you, Spirit. That was amazing," Father said.

"You are most welcome," said Spirit.

Father gave Jesus and me a quick kiss on the cheek, then motioned for us to sit. We started toward the table. Jesus pulled out my chair and assisted in pushing it in. After I was properly seated, the three sat down with me. I had never been so nervous in my entire life. There is no way I am ever going to be able to sit with these three and eat. As I sat there, I started worrying about table manners of all things. What was I going to say to them? I don't chew with my mouth open do I? Do I talk with my mouth full? Thoughts about things I have always been careful to avoid filled my mind. I hope my manners don't misbehave!

Jesus, of course, looked at me with knowledge of my thoughts and chuckled a bit. The moment he laid his hand on my shoulder, all of the nerves vanished. "Enjoy," he said, and winked.

"Lydia," Father said, "have you been enjoying the adventures we prepared for you?"

"Yes, Father. I have indeed."

"Good. Good. Glad to hear that."

I said, "Today was such a positive day for me. Everything was so uplifting. I needed that."

"Yes, you did my dear," Father says. "I am very proud

of you, you know."

"Really?"

"Well, of course. You are very special to me," Father said.

Jesus added, "You are so much harder on yourself than you should be."

I replied, "Listen, I have attended church since I was nine years old. I know with certainty I fall short of all that is expected of me."

Father said, "Ahhh, would that be your *interpretation* of our expectations or rather, what we, pointing at Jesus and the Spirit, intended for you?"

"To be honest, I thought what I was taught was your intention for me," I said, very curious now.

At that moment, shimmering mists entered the room. They were in human form, but very transparent. They rushed the table, but were gone as quickly as they had appeared. I watched the doorway to see them depart, but they vanished in thin air before reaching the door. I looked back to the other three and, as I did, I noticed the table was full of food.

"Wow. I need this at home," I said, realizing I may be more comfortable than I should be, saying something like that in front of them.

The three laughed and Father said, "Yum. This looks delectable." Father picks up one of the bowls and starts serving himself. Looking up, he said, "Dig in!"

We immediately picked up the bowls in front of us and began serving ourselves. I had no clue what I was eating, because I didn't recognize a thing. We passed the bowls around the table, enjoying small chatter as we served ourselves.

Out of habit, I wanted a prayer to be said over the meal, but I didn't know who we would pray to since everyone was here. So I asked, "Jesus, would you handle the prayer?" My funny bone wondered what would happen if he said, "Good food, good meat, good God, let's eat?"

Jesus looked at me with a smile and said, "I'll handle this one. Thank you anyway."

Oh, shoot! He can hear me! OOPS. I smiled back and said, "Yes, you had better handle this one."

With the father opposite me, we reached out to hold one another's hand before Jesus prayed, "May blessing and nourishment pour over our food and bodies. In all, our hearts let us be thankful. Amen." After that, a feeling of euphoria filled my body and soul with a deep, abiding love. I knew this was going to be the best meal I could ever eat.

During dinner, small talk filled the air. We discussed the great food. They asked about Christi, and I talked about our lives and how we were doing. They gave me some insights on how to view another's differences. Listen in love was the prevailing theme. Love, they told me, is the absence of judgment. Don't listen with ready-made opinions, but always listen in silence, thinking, I want the best for this person. Is what I want or saying, good for them? Great advice for me, having been abused, my experiences have taught me that controlling is often the only way I feel safe.

Father said, "You do that out of self-preservation, Lydia. There is nothing wrong with it, unless it prevents you from being completely open to giving and receiving love."

I asked, "How can I tell if it is holding me back? It has become a way of life now. My life, after all, didn't turn out the way I had dreamed it would."

"Lydia, give love. If it is returned, great. If it is not,

you have lost nothing. They have lost because your love is from a wonderful place! All forms of love are important, he said as he laid his hand on Jesus' arm. Sometimes we must love those who do not know how to love us back. There is no greater love than to love without condition, expecting nothing in return."

I looked at Jesus and, for the first time, I saw the scars on his hands. I hadn't noticed them on our previous visits.

I said, "There are only two people that I can recall loving completely, and without fear, and that is Jesus, and my daughter."

Father said, "If you have loved My Son, you have loved Me."

I asked, "Father, may we go back to the earlier discussion regarding interpretation of the word?"

He responded, "Yes, what is it dear?"

"You asked whether it was my interpretation or your interpretation. How can I know the difference?"

Jesus jumped in and said, "Those who spend time with us in prayer and study the word. Ask. As your knowledge and truth grows, so too does your faith. If you fail to increase your knowledge and truth, your faith may diminish, producing doubt and uncertainty in love. I describe it as feeding the soul."

I replied, "I grew up with the church, I do feel I know your word. I didn't limit myself to just the church. I explored every opportunity, even outside the church, to know you."

Father said, "Lydia, I know you did, but, if you look carefully, you'll see that your heart was scarred with so much hurt, you did not know how to allow the Spirit all the way in. Let me ask you, did you feel love and warmth and trust in us as you studied?"

"Well, I read *about* your love, but I must admit I didn't always *feel* it in my life. You know, I guess I had an ample supply of excuses: the abuse, the struggle of single parenting, sometimes working two jobs just to make ends meet. In truth, I felt alone a great deal of the time."

"Jesus said, "How do you think you might have felt had you turned to me and trusted that I was with you? We know you love us, Lydia. You always have. I just don't think you always trusted that we loved you, too. That is deep love and faith. And that is what you seek. We hope your coming here will help you find your way."

"Oh, trust me. If I never believed you loved me

131

before, I do now. I have never in my life felt more loved than I do sitting at this table right now. Oh no, please forgive me. Here I go again, getting all teary eyed. As you know, I always cry in sweet, emotional moments. Do you think you could fix that in me (looking at God)? I'm just too darn sentimental."

In unison, they said, "That is what we love about you."

My heart felt like it was bursting through my chest with the love it held for them. The Holy Spirit, lifting from his seat, attempting not to change his form, said, "When, or if, you are back on earth, think of me as air. When you need love, take a deep breath. Breathe me in. Do it now," he instructs.

I took a very deep breath, closed my eyes and savored the moment. I could feel air entering my nostrils and fill my being. The oxygen, or whatever it was, overwhelmed my senses. I sat there in peace as I thought about the three of them. A warmth traveled through my body. I think I was glowing. The peace and joy running through every pore of my being released me. I opened my eyes to see all three looking at me, smiling. They were holding hands as if it took the three of them to make it happen.

"Beautiful," I said.

The Holy Spirit said, "Remember this moment. I am with you every day in life, just like that. Believe. Keep the faith."

"I most certainly will. That felt wonderful. So peaceful."

Father said, "Well, would you look at this? It's my favorite dessert." He took a big bite of something that had a vanilla and chocolate look to it.

I took a bite. Though I cannot say what it was, it tasted even better than vanilla or chocolate. "If you tell me this has no calories, I will die," I said jokingly.

Jesus said, "Careful with your words my love. Don't forget, you are in heaven."

We all died (pun) laughing, and ate until we were stuffed.

The time had come for dinner to end. I didn't want it to. We stood up and moved to one end of the table where we gave big hugs to each other. I still felt calm, even though I had just dined with the Trinity. Wow. What a story to tell!

The Father and the Holy Spirit said their good byes and left. Jesus took my hand. We walked to the foyer where he gave me a warm kiss on the cheek and said good night. Before he left, he promised he would see me tomorrow. Poochie was waiting for me, so I decided to take a short walk outside before retiring. You know, just in case *she* needed to go.

I walked outside to see a marvelous sight. The moon was out. It's light showered the landscape. The stars were glowing ever so brightly. I took another deep breath. The same feeling I experienced earlier entered my soul. Thank you, Father, for this wonderful blessing. I let Poochie sit with me on the steps for a while, before gathering myself and my thoughts to go inside and up to bed. Before I knew it, after saying my prayers, I was sound asleep.

17

THE JUDGMENT

Early the next morning, I woke feeling refreshed. I lay back in bed to ponder the day before. Who in their right mind would ever believe I had dinner with God, Jesus, and the Holy Spirit? Not me, for sure. Yet it did happen. What an exciting night it was.

As I rolled to get up, I saw a long white gown and robe hanging at the end of my bed. I thought to myself, I don't remember seeing that last night. I was tired, so it was probably there. I just didn't notice it. I got out of bed and walked to the gown. Normally, I would take a shower but, for some reason, I put the gown and robe on. The gown was somewhat thicker than the robe, which I thought unusual. Normally, the robe is thicker. Nonetheless, I walked out onto the balcony, peered at the scene and thought, another perfect morning. It looked like rain had fallen last night. Maybe I died and went to heaven. Oh, that's right, I am in heaven. I didn't hear a thing. There's no denying the balcony was wet. Surely it rained.

I went down stairs for a closer look, only to find my

Guardian Angel, Specter, waiting on me. "Good morning, Lydia," he said, taking my hand as I got to the bottom step.

"Good morning. What's on the agenda today?" I asked, thinking he would know since he was already here.

His only word was "Judgment."

It took me back a moment. No, it actually startled me. "Ok," I said reluctantly. "Do I have anything to worry about?" I was thinking to myself at least one of them should have let me know about this last night.

"No," he said reassuring me.

I responded, "You are a man of few words. You are not volunteering anything here. Come on. Spill."

He smiled at me and takes my arm to walk out the front door.

I said, "Wait. I need to change. I have on a gown and a robe."

He said, "You are appropriately dressed."

When we walked outside, I could see a puff of clouds at the end of the long sidewalk. We walked straight to it, and entered the cloudy material. Entering, we found ourselves in a totally different place. It resembled a Cathedral. An imperial looking room that reminded me of a great church, a church similar to the one Prince Charles and Lady Di or Prince William and Kate married in.

Finally, Spirit Specter began explaining. He told me, "Before you are allowed to enter into judgment, you must go through sanctification and purification."

"How do I do that?" I asked, not having a clue what that meant.

He replied, "You will be prayed over. Hands laid on you, and you will be cleansed."

"Ok. Just tell me what to do."

He walked me to an altar, and I was laid on a porcelain table. Immediately, a choir of heavenly angels began to sing, with voices, out of this world! Instruments of every sound reverberated within the four walls. I relaxed and let the music dissolve every thought from my head and heart. All I could hear were the voices and the instruments, and it soothed me.

Lying there, I got the sense Angels were approaching me. There were no wings. Yet, the radiance and brilliance of their features told me they were of a higher order. They began a ritual of holding their hands over my body, as if to scan it. They laid their hands on my brain, my heels, and my heart. Initially I felt it was a little frightening, but actually, it felt as if I was getting a massage, only better. I felt, at times, as if pulsating currents ran through my body. Weird, right? No. It was energizing.

Afterward, I was led to a room with a large bath. Not a bathtub. This basin was three times the size of a bathtub. The water was glistening so brightly, I had difficulty looking at it. Specter explained it was holy water.

"You mean I get to bathe in Holy Water?"

"No, not bathe. Purify," he explained.

Two Angels removed the outer robe, and proceeded to walk me into the water. The soothing choirs sang in the background. It sounded as if a marching band was walking me to the waters. Entering the water, I now understood why the gown was thicker than the robe. Amazingly, the gown did not get soaked or cling to my skin in the water. It simply laid straight all the way to the bottom of my feet.

As I washed my face with the water, I felt all of my pores open up to breathe. The water was clearing every impurity in my flesh. My whole body was purified, even my hair. I was now refreshed, renewed, and regenerated. I can't help but wonder if this is the way the blind man felt when Jesus sent him to wash his eyes so that he might have sight again?

It wasn't long before the Angels walked me out to the other side. My gown was dry. My hair now gleamed. My robe was placed back on me before we proceeded through another set of doors.

This room resembled a court room. In the front, where the judge's bench might be, were three thrones of equal size and shape. On the outside ends of the outer thrones, stood two men in armor. I thought, as I looked at them, that one could be Michael the Archangel. I studied them hoping to get a response. Nothing doing, they were in warrior mode. They reminded me of the very somber guards at the Tomb of the Unknown Soldiers. I was placed directly in front of the middle throne behind a waist high table. My Guardian Angel, Specter, stood at my side, off to the right.

A horn sounded. In walked Jesus, the Holy Spirit, and the Father. The three of them looked different today. Last night, Father looked like a gentle, older man, similar to a grandfather. Today, as I look at him, I see a different view every time he moves. Today he is more light than man. I am sure this is his true God form: light, love, peace, joy, power, leader, teacher, and father. Jesus and the Holy Spirit appeared the same way. Today they emanated glory.

God spoke first.

"Lydia, you are here to be judged by the life you have lived and to determine your heavenly status. Has the life you lived provided spiritual growth and understanding? Has it propelled you to a higher understanding and commitment to your belief and mission to serve humanity? Has your life represented your heavenly devotion to the light?" Continuing, he tells me, "We have reviewed your life upon your return, and find there is much to discuss. We cannot presently judge you unconditionally as you are not certain your life on earth is complete. Once you decide your earthly life is complete, we will judge you on your merits at that point. Jesus, however, has already judged you perfect in his eyes. He loves you and he provides insight to your pain and suffering on your behalf. It is now your duty to decide if your purpose is complete on earth, or if you are ready to come home. This is your home, Lydia. Your memory has not been fully opened to understand, because your body is still functioning in an earthly realm, but please know this is your home. You must know how special you are to us. You have been given a gift, Lydia. Please do not waste it. "

His pause initiated a response from me. "I will do my best not to disappoint you. I ask for your love, guidance, and tender mercy as I seek the answer to my earthly existence. I leave here with deep regret that I did not accomplished more in this life. I promise that a lesson has been learned, even if I decide to stay. Already I have learned that I was never alone on this journey. The Holy Spirit, as well as Specter, has been with me at all times. Jesus was forever in my heart and soul. You and your love made me who I am. All of my good parts were you. This I know. I also know I allowed the pain and suffering of this life to get in the way of me being love. With this experience, I now know if I want to be a part of this heavenly existence, I must first and foremost have faith, hope, and love. I truly understand the greatest of these is love."

"Well said, my child. Now, finish your journey here. Find the answers you seek. Be blessed in your endeavors, until we meet again in that love."

I looked over at Jesus who nods his head to me in approval. I don't know why, but I love him the most. I fear God, who I see as teacher, ruler and judge. I can't quite get to know the Holy Spirit because he is not as forthcoming as Jesus. He communicates more in silence.

So I truly don't know him like I know Jesus. Jesus shares my humor and I feel that he gets me. He loves me no matter what I do or say. I love his demeanor, his presence, his radiance, and his unquestionable commitment to me. But what I suddenly knew as I stood there thinking, is that the three are one, so I really do love them all.

18

LESSONS TO LEARN

Specter escorted me back to the house, assuring me all had gone well. It is, at this point, time for lunch. I go into the dining area to find a light lunch waiting for me. I picked up a glass of water with the plate and go to the main living area where I had earlier met with Chad, mom, and dad. After walking into the elaborate room, I ate my lunch and looked around. The small table with photos now had a picture of Brad and me, a picture of me playing with Poochie out back and of course, mom, dad, and Chad. I can't help but return to my thoughts about what Brad had said about this being our home one day. "One day," I said out loud. Now that I had returned to see Christi, I am no longer so sure of my decision any more. Do I return to finish my life, holding no fear of death and abuse, or do I stay here where I know I shall finally be at peace? Decisions, decisions, decisions.

The instant I sat in one of the Queen Anne chairs, the Gentleman came in to tell me I had a visitor. I thanked him for his gracious kindness and asked him to show them in. In walked a woman who announced herself as Distonia.

As the Gentleman excused himself, I handed him my empty plate and glass. "Can I get you something to drink?" I offered to Distonia.

"No, thank you," she replied smiling.

"Well, Distonia, what brings you here?" I said, motioning for us to sit.

"I am here to educate you on your journey," she replied.

I asked, "And what journey would this be?"

"Intransitive travel," she replied.

"What exactly does this involve?"

Distonia explained, "Since you are not able to accomplish this journey on your own, because of your situation, particularly since death has not occurred, we will need to use alternative methods to show you how an individual chooses their next life. Normally, you would go into the future area and choose for yourself the life and lesson you wish to experience next. However, you are not fully judged so we do not know your precise level. During judgment, you are typically assigned a level. Some lose a level, while others stay at the same level or increase their level of light. After judgment, you are given time to educate yourself on your new level and see the options for future endeavors you wish to experience. Since those things did not occur, we will permit you to only watch a previous scenario of different lives."

I said, "That makes sense. I was not given my level, so we don't know what to review."

She continued, "I am also not able to inform you of your current status because you do not have full memory capacity at this time. That would be tearing down barriers that we do not wish to dismantle."

I responded, "Understood."

She asked if I was ready, and I replied, "Yes."

We stood as she became a blue sparkling light and began swirling around me. I felt like I was beginning to get used to this now. Previously, I felt a little off balance with vertigo. It was easier now.

When we came to a stop, we were in a video room. There was a massive screen on the wall with large comfortable seating in front of it. There was a rise to the seats that allowed us to be positioned directly in the middle of the big screen. We walked up the steps to take our seats. She reached in a compartment beside her seat and pulled out a long box. She waved her hand and four distinct lighting areas lit up. She places it in front of me and explains. "Each of these lights represents a life you will be able to view to learn a new lesson. What you will see here today are the options you had when you chose the life you are in now."

"Oh, good! I really would love to see that," I replied.

She instructed me to lay my hand on the first light. I laid my hand on it and a beaming light pierces my hand. The screen in front of me lights up.

The first life is the one I am living. It depicts pretty much everything I had reviewed up to this point over the last few days. I relived every emotion just as before, connecting to pain and happiness. She pulled my hand off when the review ended.

"So, the lesson, assigned to this life was to learn giving with no expectation of receiving, to serve with a grateful heart. I would say that is exactly what has happened in this life. Interesting lesson," I replied.

She puts my hand on the second light.

The screen lights up. It shows my birth and progress through life. I am ultimately a psychiatrist in this life. It shows the struggles I go through to complete the education needed to achieve this career. Although my family was financially well off, I didn't have supportive parents, at all, during my years achieving the goals. The threat of removing financial support was always in the forefront from parents who were mostly interested in grades and achievements. Outward appearances looked great, but the stress levels were enormous. I felt all the struggles I would have to go through to attain the objective. The movie showed me with a successful therapy practice. It seemed to zone in on a particular patient.

Distonia again pulls my hand off the light, then moves it to the third light.

On the third light, it shows my birth and progress through life. I am a precious little girl. I am overly loved by parents who fought hard to have me. Through the whole experience, there was difficulty in becoming pregnant, and the journey was full of happiness upon my birth. They cherished and loved me dearly. I was spoiled beyond imaginable degrees. On my sixteenth birthday, I was given a brand new car. With a new driver's license in hand, my parents happily handed me the keys. I left the driveway waving goodbye to my parents as they stood arm and arm watching me drive away. Both were smiling from ear to ear. Two hours later, I was dead.

I screamed, "Oh, my! I was so caught up in the wonderful story when the accident happened, I was shocked to see how it ends. How sad! I wanted to cry. It affected me so much. The poor girl! Oh, her parents must be devastated."

Distonia said, "There is a lesson in every life. Life is fleeting, so we must make each day count." She takes my hand and places it on the fourth and final light.

The light emits through my hand. I am still in heaven, sitting in classrooms being taught by leaders of the hierarchy. I am given classes on how to communicate with light emissions, how to swirl and travel through heaven. I go into space, and end up on a planet where I am told I must create and sustain life. I must create gravity, space, and time. Then I must decide the type of sentient beings that will live there. Afterwards, I must create universal laws to govern the planet and the beings who call it home. Each goal is designed to help me make it as perfect a world as I can create. It will be judged by God himself.

I said, after she removes my hand, "Wow, that is the one I should have chosen."

Distonia replied, "That work comes with great

responsibility. You did not feel you were ready for that mission yet."

I responded, "Well, that makes sense. That would be a tough job. I am confused though. I thought God is the creator of all universes. How would I be able to create a life planet?

Distonia replied, "You are correct. You are the vessel he uses to do the work. God already knows how to do all of this. He uses you to produce his wishes. You must understand if he does not approve, it would become nonexistent."

"Oh, ok. Through him all things are possible. I get it now."

"Exactly," she said. She puts away the box and motions for us to leave. We walk down the stairs and, upon reaching the bottom, she begins to swirl. We are soon back in my living room as before.

I thanked her for the journey and she wished me blessings before she left. I walked outside. Poochie was running through the yard chasing something that looked like a stick. I looked around the edge of the house to see mom sitting in a gazebo. Dad had thrown the stick for Poochie to chase and was yelling, "Get it, girl!"

I walked over to them and sat down beside mom. I put my arms around her. She laid her hand on my leg and asked, "Full day?"

"Yes mom, and an interesting one, too."

She said, "Isn't it great how it all works?"

"I know, mom. When you left, I was so devastated. I had no clue of the adventure you were about to go on."

Mom replied, "Well, the thing is, when I came back, I came back deceased. I regained my heavenly memory back very quickly. For you, he is showing you heaven in a special way. You can now go back to life and know there is more."

"Mom, people are going to think I'm crazy if I go back and tell them about all of this."

Mom said, "Honey, the important fact you have to keep in mind is that it is more important to be close to the light than it is to be close to earthly views. Everyone has their own deity or light. For some, it is Buddhism, Christianity, or cults. There are many different views. Remain focused on the personal relationship you have with the light or your truth. Focus on your growth and your beliefs. Be respectful of others feeling always, but never sway when it comes to gaining understanding from what you experience. Let love be your guide. One day, they will see the light and know all you now know. This is going to make you a better person. You will always know to act in love."

"Gosh, you are right, mom." I looked around and said, "What is dad doing over there?"

"He's cooking a variety of foods for dinner," she said.

"Oh, that sounds good," I said rubbing my belly.

We sat for a while before Dad, Chad, Brad, mom, and I go to a big picnic table to eat the wonderfully prepared food. I asked Dad, "Why does everything here taste so much better?"

He laughed and replied, "We have the ultimate recipe here," as he shoots his eyebrows up in mischief reply.

I looked around the table at the perfect scene. My family and Brad are here with me. Thinking out loud, I said, "Well, I wonder what comes next.

19

CLEARING THE MIND

We sat there until long after dark. The sunset was amazing. The glow of the sun beams fell silently across the pond into the dark of night. A warm gentle breeze blew through our hair and across our faces. The flowers had a sweet aroma that filled our senses. As darkness began appearing, the night sky was sprinkled with stars, which seemed to sparkle and glimmer radiance. The moon was so large, I felt I could reach out and touch it. We had all eaten heartily in this beautiful space and were now filled both inside and out from the food and beauty. I looked at Poochie laying at my feet and bent over to rub her. She looked at me with those puppy dog eyes full of contentment. She had a full belly, too.

Mom, Dad, and Chad said their good nights and left. Brad and I sat on the deck chair together and watched as the moon rose to light the night sky.

"Brad," I said, "Wouldn't it have been wonderful if we could have had this life on earth? That we could do it all over again and you wouldn't die?" Without waiting for a reply, I continued. "The picture would be so complete with Christi here." After a short pause I added, Brad, what should I do? I feel so content here. The struggles in life there, compared to here, are night and day.

Brad looks around at our home, then looks back at me and says, "the decision is yours alone. I am sure you will make the right decision. All you have to remember is that Jesus told us never to be content with earthly things, so cherish this moment, this gift. I love you, Lydia. Always have. Always will. Even through eternity."

"I love you, too," I replied with a tone of certainty that I have never felt before. We kissed, then continued talking about all that has happened up until now.

Brad told me, "You have been through every step that I know of for entry. I can't think of anything else you could view."

"I know. That scares me," I replied. "Jesus could tell me it is time for my decision, and I am not ready to give one. I know where I would rather be, but to leave Christi would be so hard for me. She needs me, plus, I've been told there are things I still need to do on earth. Do I stay or do I go back? Is the lesson Christi, or the message I need to share?"

Brad pondered a moment, puts his arm around me, before saying, "God will guide you."

"Yes, I believe that too. I trust him so much now."

Brad stood and began gathering up things to put away. He closed the grill, and put the doggie toys in the crate. We strolled up the walk and climbed the steps to the house. He kissed me good night, then walked away. I know this is terrible of me, but I wanted him to stay. Even as I thought it, I said to myself, "This is heaven, Lydia!" The thought was not in terms of fornication, but love. I loved feeling so close to him. To be inseparable, you know, becoming as one. But, he was gone. I went inside to climb the steps to my room with Poochie at my heels. "We're inseparable, aren't we girl?" I said to Poochie.

I arrived in my room and went straight for the shower. I stood there with the warm water cascading over me, relaxing me. I later climbed into bed feeling wonderful. A day I won't soon forget. I said my prayers and slept deeply throughout the night.

The next morning I awoke to the light streaming into my room. I got up and threw on the robe lying at the end of my bed. I walked downstairs and headed toward the dining area. My breakfast was waiting for me on the balcony. I went out through the double doors in the dining area and sat at the table prepared for me. I ate wheat cereal, and some fruit. After I ate, I sat, somewhat perplexed, not knowing what to do. Just as I was about to go inside, Specter walked out on the balcony and sat in the chair next to me.

"Good Morning, Lydia."

"Good Morning, Specter. So, what is on my agenda for today?"

He looked at me and smiled that all knowing smile and replied, "First, you are just going to relax and enjoy the morning. Walk around, view the area, and try to decide what you plan to do about returning."

"That's a good idea. I really haven't slowed down enough to think things through and weigh the consequences of my choices going forward. I hope everyone knows how much this has meant to me. Thank you for your help," I said, as I lay my hand over his.

He replied, "You are quite welcome," as he laid his other hand over mine.

We parted with a hug, then I went back upstairs to change. It was strange how every time I opened the door to the closet, well-fitting clothes were hanging there. Today, I threw on a white top with three-quarter-length sleeves and a pair of dark green casual slacks. I threw a green and white scarf around my neck and tied it in the front. Lying on the closet floor was a pair of sandals that fit perfectly. They were very comfortable, with cushioned soles that would be great for the walk I intended to take. Seeing these clothes made me think of the night gown I was wearing upon my arrival. Thank God I am not having to walk around in that, I thought.

Leaving my room, I looked at Poochie and said, "Come on, girl." We walked outside to a gorgeous day. I walked among the pathways and mazes of beautiful plants, flowers, and trees. The plants seemed to turn to look at me as I passed. I am so happy here. I walked down a path to find Jesus talking to Brad.

"Well, hello there," Jesus said. Brad walked over to me and kissed me on the cheek.

"I am so glad the two of you are here," I said. "Jesus, I have a question for you."

He asked very playful, "Just one?"

"Well, many, but just one right now," I laughed.

He said, "Ok, shoot."

I asked, "If I stay here, will I be here with my family in my home and happy like it was last night?"

Jesus replied with a question, "Heaven is your perfect world. Was last night perfect?"

I replied, "Yes."

"Then, that is your heaven," he said.

I looked at Brad, "Was last night your perfect heaven?"

"I think you know the answer to that one," he smiled. "YES!"

After a few more silly exchanges, I asked Jesus to talk to me about his time on earth. What the world meant to him? He talked about growing up with a carpenter for a father and learning the trade. He said he enjoys working with wood. The smell of the wood is exhilarating to him. It is life in his hands. What the wood becomes out of his molding becomes a story. He talked about the disciples and their personalities. He said, "Many think that Judas is despised for betraying me. When in fact, what many do not know is that he *chose* the life of betrayal. That was hard for him. It was hard for the world, yet, it was his gift to me and the world. Someone had to betray me. How else would I fulfil God's desire for me to redeem mankind? Judas is special to me."

I looked at him, stunned. "You're right. Everyone has to choose a life that will teach, no matter the cost. His lesson of betrayal came at a steep price. Wow, when viewing life from earth, we often fail to see the deeper lesson behind every action, especially hurtful actions." I looked at him in deep thought, I stopped to ask, "Do you think my stepfather chose the life to abuse others?"

"Of course," Jesus replied. "Once you get full memory back, Lydia, you will understand, and you will have peace about it. We all learn through the experiences."

"I prayed so often, Jesus. The lesson I was learning, was that God didn't hear me through my suffering. Isn't there another way to teach lessons that allow all of us to feel your closeness and protection?"

Jesus looked at me and said, "You are not promised a pain-free life. If we rush in to correct everything, the chosen lessons will not be taught. We do not create these events, but we are there to see you through them. As you grow in love and understanding, you will learn this. In your weakness, you felt abandoned by me, but that was far from the truth. Because of your deep love, you managed to find your way back. In full understanding, what your stepfather did to you made you the wonderful person you are now. What does the song say? Count it all joy. Also, think back to your favorite plaque that hangs in your home, FOOTPRINTS. When you saw only one set of Footprints, it was then that I carried you."

Jesus continued, "Lydia, we understand you so much more than you understand yourself. For instance, some may think that because of your perfect home here, with fine furnishings, large and grand, that you are materialistic, when in fact, it is the opposite. We understand the house represents the lack that you suffered on earth. By having that home, you find security and peace. No stress, no clutter, only the joy that you find in it with your family. It was written, in my house are many mansions. This home is by no means a mansion in heaven, but it **is** your mansion. Some may also think that having Brad here is still a human need. The one thing you lost and could not find again after Brad's death was love. Brad being here is completing the circle of love in your life. You had the child, but lost the father. Having Brad here, completes that circle for you. He also recounted the forty two cents for food. There was always worry about having enough money to eat and survive. The Gentleman at the nursing home serving as your greeter is another significant result. You went out of your way to bring him candy in the nursing home, because he tugged at your heart strings. He watched over your mother. You, having him here in your perfect heaven, also, represented you still wanting to help him, even though he needs no help in heaven. He thought you were special in life, too. You affected him, showed him love when he needed it. He holds great esteem here in heaven, being a greeter, just as I am your teacher. Now, you have completed the journey of heaven that, for you, wasn't completed on earth. It is still a lesson that you continue to learn, even here. True love never ends; it is a circle."

I stopped, looked at Jesus, and said, "I understand." I turned to Brad and asked, "Don't you have any questions for him? Like, why he took you from me, and that without me, you are nothing?" I smiled and pushed Brad a little, trying to lighten the mood with a joke.

Jesus shot back at me, "What about me? Don't forget me," pretending to be jealous. We all laughed, so I pushed Jesus, too. He stumbles like he was going to fall off a cliff.

I looked at him and smiled. "You are so easy to love, unlike me. You love me with all of my faults. You have no faults, so there is no problem loving perfection. But, me. Oh, you have your hands full!"

He grabbed me and hugged me and said, "Oh yes, I do!"

I asked, "Well, as wonderful as this moment is, I need to get back to the house. Do the two of you want to go back with me?"

Brad replied, "No, Jesus and I have some unfinished business to discuss." He gave me a quick peck on the lips before he and Jesus wondered off in conversation.

I yelled, "Don't talk about me the whole time!" We all laughed and I turned back to the path to the house. Once back, I go to the library. Waiting for me is the Holy Spirit.

I asked, "How did you know that I needed to see you?"

He said, "I am all knowing," and smiles.

"My question is this. If I should choose to stay, how will I get this knowledge back to my family?"

"You mean document everything here, right?"

I replied, "Yes."

He waved his hand and a book appeared. "It is written."

I picked up the book and read the cover. LYDIA'S GIFT. I opened it. The words on the page were written by me. Everything appeared as if I had sat down myself and had hand written every word. I went to the back page and the last section ended with me walking into this library. I looked up at the Holy Spirit and said, "How will they know the end?"

He replied, "The words are added to the page as you live it. I told you, this is not earth; this is heaven. Things happen differently here."

I said, "Yes, I see that. If I stay, will I be able to go back to give them the book?"

"Yes, you will have the opportunity to finish whatever you decide. If you go back, you will divinely channel all of this (he points at the book) for the benefit of others. If you decide to stay, you will take this with you, to give to your family before you die. It will all work out. This is not our first rodeo you know, we have done this before," and he smiled.

"Whoa! That is the first time I have heard you get spunky, humorous! Cool. You have just put my mind, heart, and soul at peace. I know my decision."

20

A CELEBRATON OF LOVE

Feeling at peace with my decision, I left the library. I knew what I wanted to do now. I walked up to my room to get ready for the celebration Brad had mentioned earlier. I went to the room expecting my clothing, to be as before, waiting on me. This time, there was nothing. A decision was made. The outfit I have on will have to do.

I walked down the stairs to find my dad waiting on me. "Hi, dad. Well, look at you, all gussied up," I said to him grabbing the arm he held out for me on the last step. "I think I may be a little under dressed," looking down to compare my clothes to his.

Dad's reply was "Ah, you look beautiful, honey."

We walked out the front door and to my amazement, the yard was full of people. It seemed everyone I had met at the first dinner was there. Jeffrey, Liddy, Chad, mom, and old friends that had come to dinner that night stood watching as we walked out. Others I had not met previously were also there. I swear, I think I even saw Joseph with his coat of many colors.

Dad said, "Are you ready?"

I had grown used to the unexpected, so instead of asking for what, I just said, "Yes, I am."

As we stepped onto the sidewalk, the crowd parted, opening a pathway down the middle of the gathering. At the end of the pathway, stood Brad. He looked more handsome than ever. His glow was visibly brighter. His smile was directed only to me and in that moment, I knew this whole night was about our love for each other.

I looked at dad and said again, "Yes, I'm ready, definitely ready. I have been waiting for this moment my entire life."

He squeezed my hand and began walking me forward down the pathway.

Music began the moment we started walking. I looked around because I couldn't tell where the music was coming from. The more they sang, the louder they sang, the brighter the glow on my skin became. Suddenly my clothes began changing into a long beautiful flowing gown. As I walked, I could see the material climbing my skin to effortlessly adorn my body, replacing the earlier outfit. The material was white in color with sparkles embedded in it. The sparkles were not on the material, but somehow in the material. With each step I took, the gown seemed to come more alive. I thought to myself, it must be blinding everyone because it's so bright. As we proceeded, the gown seemed to move in slow motion, falling back and forth with each step. By the time I reached Brad, I was fully adorned for the occasion. I felt absolutely radiant. My emotions were in full chaos; love, happiness, wonder, and excitement filled the air.

My father handed my hand to Brad, and gave me a kiss on the cheek. Brad took both of my hands in his. The skin on our hands were radiating light. Our hands seemed to be meshed as one in the light form. I felt the heat from his light in the palms of my hands. He looked at me and said, "Jesus has allowed us to commit our love to one another in front of our family and friends. Lydia, our love has reached above life itself. We have become love, soul mates if you will. In front of God, Jesus, the Holy Spirit, our friends, family, and our daughter, I commit myself to you."

His words were a shock to me! "Our daughter?" I looked to my right and standing with my mother was Christi! "How could this be? How is she here?"

Jesus whispered to me that she is having a dream and is attending through her dream state. Nothing could be more perfect. I looked at her and almost lost it. I wanted to jump up and down with the joy bursting from my heart. I now know full love and joy. Never before had I experienced such delight in every breath taken. I am breathing love. Jesus looked delighted, embracing the moment with the kind of love only he could provide. As he witnessed our union, the music seemed to rise and fall to each of my heart beats, so full and expanding.

The chorus was Ahh ahhh ahhhh, ahhh ahhh ahhhh, AHHH AHHH AHHHH!

Building with each moment of joy, this music lit up the yard and even the air. I turned to Christi and we looked at each other with total understanding of the moment. She could read my thoughts and I could read hers. "This is your father, Christi."

She shook her head in understanding. All was perfectly right with our family; her father, her mother, and child had finally become whole. Brad was no longer a memory, but part of us. This is the final understanding God gave to me about life and love. Even though Brad had left me with child, his love had not departed me. She is a gift of our love, one that will endure beyond earth; it is immortal.

The music changed and a traditional celebratory dance

began. Brad and I take each other's hands and follow the inside of our arms up, with the outside of the hand passing the cheek. We do the opposite hand the same way, running up the inside of the arm, past the cheek, both arms held up in the air. We took turns running our hands over the outer edge of the head and down the shoulders. He does it first, and then I followed, showing me how it is done. I pull my hands to me, as if I am pulling his spirit out of his body into mine. He took me in his arms and we began a celebration waltz. I couldn't believe my feet were keeping in step with his. The music and our dance rotation began slowly. As we increased the rotation, the guests began doing the same. The waltz between couples was perfectly in sync with other couples. I felt we were gliding and the music was carrying us away into the joy and splendor of the moment.

When the music stopped, we were appropriately in front of Jesus who formally blessed our union. The events of the rest of the night began with clapping and celebration, as everyone came up to hug each of us. I looked around for Christi, but couldn't find her. I went to mom and she said, "She left honey. She had to go back."

I said, "Awh! I wanted her to meet Brad."

Mom said, "She did honey. Before you came out, they

spent some time together. She said she liked him very much. She said she had never seen you so happy."

"Oh, I am mom! So very happy!"

The rest of the night was walking around with Brad talking to all who were there. At the close of the evening, an event took place that would take anyone's breath away.

Jesus and the Holy Spirit came to where Brad and I were sitting and sat with us. The sky brightened as light events streamed from one side to the other. Not fireworks, but dancing light. Music was playing again and angels appeared in various colors. Some were glowing white, some were pale pink and others were a pale blue. Their wings were large and lifted them straight up without the struggle for steadiness at all. They did a ceremonial dance and sang in intervals of each other. The dazzling stream of light they left behind crisscrossed to create an array that grew before dispersing into a glorious explosion.

I watched Jesus. His face showed he was very much in the moment. He looked at me and winked. I heard him say, "You are so special."

Suddenly, I was no longer there. As I parted, I could see Brad getting smaller and smaller until I could see him no more.

21

FINAL DECISION

I was devastated. I was standing alone in the area where I had arrived in the beginning of my adventure. No one was there. I stood there waiting for the next event to begin from this place of nothingness. In the distance I could see the light approaching. The image was in total light form, but shaped as a man's human body. As it arrived, it became more solid. I could make out the features and, to my delight, it was Jesus.

I grabbed him and said, "Oh, I am so glad it's you. Is it time for me to leave now?"

He said, "Is it time for your gift to be over? Yes. Is it time for you to return to your life? It is up to you, we need your decision."

I looked at him and nodded my head in understanding. Before the celebration I was certain of my decision. The happiness I felt tonight would be so easy to choose; however, I cannot be selfish. I must think of Christi and the fact that she needs me. With that in mind, I said, "I need to return to earth to be with my daughter. I feel she needs me. I would not want her to suffer the same losses I did in life. She needs me to be there and I want that. I will return to you another day, Jesus, a better person than before. I love you so much."

He replied, "Well done, my child. You have loved deeply and demonstrated wise judgment in your decision. What you are showing me now is that it is wonderful to surrender to love. You put Christi's needs over your own. There is wonderful power in your gift."

I tell him, "I wish I could have you with me on earth as I did here."

"Oh, my child, but you do. Don't forget what you were taught here. Breathe me, love me in every decision you make, then I will be with you."

"I will do that in everything I do. I promise!"

I felt emotional confusion. Turmoil washed over me as I contemplated what I was now leaving and the happiness I had experienced here. I knew I was making the right decision for the child that I brought into the world. I love Christi, just as God loves his son and us. Brad will understand. We spoke about it enough when we were together here in this land of harmony and love. He would do the same. One day, we will all unite again and rejoice over what we have accomplished as a family. Christi will know her father's love. Biased as I am, I cannot find one moment of selfishness in Brad. I can't wait until we both return to see what Christi's perfect heaven is like.

Getting lost in my thoughts, I looked to Jesus and asked him to tell Brad goodbye for me.

"No need," he replied. "He knows and sees all things. He understands your heart and emotions as if they were his own."

"Good," I replied. "So let's get this over with. Before I go, though, I want to tell you how much all of this has meant to me. I have grown from this experience. Please tell me I will remember all of this."

Jesus said, "Yes, you will remember it all. Write about it, and help those who are struggling with life to see there is a greater joy here with the Father. Tell them to count all of their sorrows and pain as joy. When they have achieved their chosen mission, their light will grow brighter and deeper. Just as yours has." He looked at me with great love. He takes me in his arms and holds me close, as if he were struggling to let go of me. He finally releases and says, "It is time to go through departure." I will see you soon. With those words, he disappears just as he arrived into the light.

Lambrett who I had met earlier arrived in the company of my Holy Specter to escort me back. Lambrett asked, "Have you made a decision, Lydia? Will you be staying, or returning to your earthly existence?"

I looked at him without hesitation and answered, "I am returning to my life on earth to be with my daughter and to complete whatever it is you expect of me."

He said, "As you wish."

He backed away from me. My Holy Specter began to swirl, but stopped suddenly, as if something didn't function properly. Etched on his face was unfathomable concern. He looked from me, to directly behind me. I turned to see what caught his attention.

A spirit was sitting down the next arrival. As the swirling stopped, I could not believe my eyes. It was CHRISTI!

She looked confused, finding herself surrounded by all of the emptiness of the area. She saw me, then said, "Mom! What is going on? Where am I?"

I looked at Lambrett and my Holy Specter in question. "What is going on here?"

Her Guardian announces that she is arriving in heaven.

"I don't understand," I replied. "Is she dreaming again or is she dead?"

Lambrett replied, "Dead."

"How could this be?" I couldn't believe what I was hearing. "She is a young vibrant girl. It is too soon for her to die."

Lambrett replied, "Lydia, all are assigned their number of days. It was her time."

I wanted to run to her and hug her, to tell her she would be ok, but there was a barrier between us. "Why is this barrier here?"

Lambrett replied, "she is arriving, while you are in departure."

I began to panic, "No, I want to be with her. That is my reason for returning. I can't believe this is happening this way. She's my child. She's an adult yes, but nonetheless my child!"

"Wait, I won't go then! We can all be together here now," I exclaimed with the realization a change in my decision will resolve it.

Lambrett sighed and hesitated, "Lydia, you have already chosen to return. It cannot be reversed."

"NO!" I cry in horror.

"Lydia, once you made the decision to go, it was final," Lambrett reports. "It will be ok. You will return once you have completed your mission on earth."

"But you don't understand. It was because of Christi that I wanted to go back. If she is here, I don't need to go back! You had to know this was going to happen! Why didn't you tell me she would be here soon? I would have made the decision to stay."

My Specter replied, "Lydia, you still have a mission to complete, or God would never have let you choose to return. Remember, trusting in him is the answer. Trust him to know returning is what you need."

I looked over at Christi. She was standing there in silence, as if the heavenly clarity of death and heaven had finally arrived. Then she spoke, "They are right, Mom. You have more to do. My clarity of the situation is better than yours, because I have crossed over. You will see one day why you had to return."

With that, the Holy Specter began swirling. I felt myself traveling, moving. I felt my inner spirit getting heavier and heavier with each moment that passed. Soon, I felt myself enter my earthly body as my Holy Specter left me. There I lay in a hospital bed, just waking from a coma.

22

RETURN TO SORROW

Carly, my sister, was sitting in the chair beside my bed. When I came to, she jumped out of her chair and ran over to me. "Lydia! I am so glad you're awake," she said with unbridled excitement. "How are you feeling?"

I replied, "Like a ton of bricks were dropped on me."

She urgently runs around to the other side of my bed to retrieve the button to call the nurse. "Yes," the reply came over the speaker.

"Lydia is awake. Please get the doctor," she said anxiously. She looked back at me and asked, "Do you have a headache or anything?"

"A small one, I guess. What are all these bandages for?" I felt around my head and there were bandages covering it. The return to my body seemed to confuse me somewhat.

She told me, "You had surgery. You had an aneurism."

Suddenly the memories started flooding back. The fall in the bedroom, the black out and, yes, even my trip to heaven was becoming clearer. "Oh, that's right," I said, recalling everything.

The nurse came in and started checking my vitals. She stuck a thermometer in my mouth and a cuff on my arm to measure my blood pressure. Just as she completed the health assessment, the doctor walked in.

Dr. King said, "Welcome back, Lydia. How are you feeling?" He continued with probing questions while reading my vitals on the chart. "It is good to see you coming around so soon."

I asked, "How long have I been out?"

"Two days," he said. "How is your memory?" He started asking me who the president was, my full name, and my birth date.

I replied to all successfully. He said, "Well, looks like no permanent damage has occurred. That's a good sign."

Not for me, I thought to myself. I was feeling a bit sorry for myself knowing I had missed the opportunity to be in heaven already. I can't think about that now.

We raised up my bed into a sitting position. As Dr.

King left, Carly walked out into the hall with him. When Carly walked back in, my siblings were with her. Tom, Matt, Carly, and Jeanie sat by my bed. Carly said she needed to tell me something. Then she proceeded with the news. "Lydia, Christi was in an accident this morning."

I sat straight up and asked if she was ok, not wanting them to know yet that I already knew. They looked at each other and said, "No, Lydia. Christi didn't make it."

My first reaction was one of panic, facing the news of her death coupled with the fact she won't be here. I had given up the choice to stay in heaven, so we are again separated. My reaction to this information came off as shock instead of the realization of my dire situation and choices. My family didn't know the depths of my sorrow or what I had just been through. They saw my panic over Christi's death as normal. They had no idea how un-normal all of this was.

I began to cry. I felt so overwhelmed from the whole thing. I asked, "Where is she now?"

Matt said, "We have her at Rawlings Funeral Home."

I asked, "How did it happen?" I knew already that she had passed, but not how it had occurred.

Tom told me, "She was driving to the hospital this morning. On her way, she stopped for a school bus. The officer said a car was traveling at a high rate of speed on an adjoining street. Seeing the bus, the driver panicked and was unable to stop. He pressed the accelerator by mistake and lost total control trying to make the turn without stopping. He ran directly into the driver's side of Christi's car, killing her instantly. The impact knocked both cars in the opposite direction of children waiting for the bus. The officer said that hitting Christi saved those children."

I just couldn't wrap my head around it all. I still wanted to cry. I broke down. It was too much to take in. Everything that had happened to me these past few days was so overwhelming. I came back to be with her and now she was gone. I began sobbing. I knew God had a greater plan, but missing Christi was unbearable. Especially knowing it could have been different had I chosen to stay in heaven. I laid my head back on the bed, closed my eyes, and said to myself, "Count it all joy."

23

THE BOOK

Before everyone left that evening, I lay there contemplating life. I must admit, I was not feeling that well. My head was hurting and I found it hard to think. I thought back to the day the Holy Spirit said my book was already written. How do I find it, I wonder? Would it still be written even though I have returned?

Soon, Carly and the others said they were leaving so I could rest for a bit. She was going to go home, have a bite to eat, then return. I asked her to do me a favor. "Go to my house and look for a book. It's called, **Lydia's Gift**. If you find it, please bring it to me."

She said, "Lydia, you can't read now. You should rest."

"Oh, I know," I replied. "I just need the book, if it's there."

She shook her head at me as if to say I am hard-headed and, reluctantly, said, "Ok" before leaving.

I laid back against the propped up pillows and closed

my eyes. I soon heard someone call my name. I opened my eyes, but no one was there. I closed my eyes again, and heard the same thing, "Lydia." I opened my eyes again and just laid there in silence waiting to hear it again. When it occurred again, I laid in wait until finally I could see him. My Holy Specter was there with me. He was slowly showing himself to me. "Lydia, because of your gift, I am able to show myself to you now."

I replied, "Oh, Specter, I am so glad. I was beginning to think it had all been a dream."

He said, "Your book is in the bottom drawer of your chest."

"It is? Thank you! I needed to let Carly know where to look."

I dialed Carly. When she answered, I told her to look in the bottom drawer of my chest, then, I hung up.

I turned to look back at my Specter but he was gone. "Specter," I said hoping to get him to show himself.

He appeared standing at the foot of my bed. "Yes, Lydia?"

"Can you stay with me? I want to know that I am not crazy and that you exist," I said offering a feeble explanation for my urgent reaction to his departure. "I know I had a privileged experience, and I know what it meant to me, but will others believe it? How do I relay this miracle to others in a way they can see it? Being back on earth, gives me pause. Did it really happen?"

"I understand," he replied with a smile. "It happened, Lydia."

I told him, "It is so wonderful knowing you are here with me."

He replied, "She is fine you know. Christi is going through the process now. She is very happy, Lydia. She is spending time with Brad."

"Thank you," I said, feeling so much better that they were together. I appreciated Specter's forethought of my concern. I still find myself in mother-protective-mode. I needed to know she was ok. The excitement that she was with her father, getting to know him, was so important. God has this perfect plan for our lives. I somehow knew he was with her. I think I actually felt better about her being there, and me here, than I would if it were reversed, me there and her here. I knew she was safe in the arms of the Father. Mother bear can relax now, I thought to myself.

"She is also with your mother, father, Chad and yes Poochie too ," my Specter confided.

I am, indeed, comforted with this information. Now, I must accomplish the mission set before me, come what may. I laid my head back on the bed and, before I knew it, I had fallen asleep.

Hours later, I woke up with the nurse taking my vitals. Carly walked in just as the nurse was finishing up. The nurse asked if she could get us anything, but we didn't need a thing. In Carly's hand was the book.

"Oh, good, you found it," I said.

Carly asked, "Why is this book so important to you?"

I replied, "Sit down, Carly. I have a story to tell you. Before doing anything else, I opened the book to the last page. There is nothing there. I panic. "Oh, no! It's all lost," I said under my breath not realizing Carly could hear me.

Carly was sitting at the edge of my bed asked, "What is lost, Lydia?"

"The book! The book was written, now the words are gone!" I began telling her of my experiences. She sat there, in deep silence, listening to the whole story. I told her of my visit with Brad, mom, dad, Chad, and seeing Jeffrey and Poochie. She laughed at me seeing Poochie. "Hey, she was so important to me," I replied with a smile.

She said, "Oh, I know that. The two of you were inseparable."

I continued, "So, Carly, this book should have mentioned everything that happened to me after my black out. It described heaven, and the function of light, and how our lives are meant to help us grow in that light. Love is everywhere, Carly! Everything we do should be guided by love. I spent a lot of time with Jesus and he was so warm, kind, and humorous. He understands us completely! His love is so pure. He loves us no matter what, even with our faults. Did you know that Judas had a mission for God? Yeah, who would have betrayed Jesus if Judas hadn't accepted the role?" I was spitting out all of the things that were explained to me about heaven and how we all are cherished. She was taking it all in. It is just like Carly to be so open to understanding. I knew if anyone would believe me, it would be her.

She said, "Wow, I can't wait to read it." She has always been the big reader in the family. She could get through a whole book in a day sometimes. She took the book from my hand and begins flipping through the empty pages. "Lydia, are you sure this is the right book?"

I replied, "I don't know why the words are no longer on the pages. I am supposed to share this great lesson. I assume I will have to re-write it," I say as I flipped through the empty pages. I looked over at Specter and he smiled. "God allowed me to see all of it. He wanted me to share my experience with the world. He wants everyone to know of his great love. Believing, having faith, and functioning in love can bring answers to a hurt world. It is a gift that he is allowing me to deliver. I am so honored."

She replied, "That may be so, but some might think you are unstable you know?"

I said, "This is one time I am not concerned. I love the light, first and foremost, in all things. Oh, you wait, Carly! You will be awestruck at what you read. You will know God loves you by the way he treated me. Each one of us is unique. God loves us for our uniqueness. He relates to us on our own level. Oh," I said getting excited, "we each have our own perfect heaven. Wait until you read what mine is."

I was getting so wound up in the discussion. My head began hurting again, so I lay back on the bed. She said, "Relax a bit. Take a nap."

I said, "I think I will."

I went to sleep, thinking of my adventures in heaven and how God will help me put the words within reach of others. I rest assured he will guide me.

24

JOURNEYS END

After leaving the hospital, I went home and began the process of documenting my heavenly journey. My Holy Specter reminded me that God said he would inspire me of the words for this book. Specter now appears only when I call for him. It is great to have this option for venting ideas and thoughts. My family is in disbelief that I can see him. I think they feel the aneurism has affected my brain in some way. I tell them that I agree. It has made me more open to the Spiritual world. I was given a gift. I see life's struggles now with new meaning. I don't have the beaten down feeling anymore. The trials are opportunities for lessons I chose to learn in this life. These lessons will help my light grow and become brighter, which is my ultimate goal. Some may interpret this book as belief in reincarnation, opposing the Christian belief. What I believe, however, is that Jesus was resurrected and came back to us again. Was he reincarnated? Did he die and come back to life? I say yes. Is that reincarnation? Don't know. What I do believe is that all things are possible through Jesus. Does this fictional book portray possibilities? Yes. I hope imaginations open up to inspire visions of the many wonders of heaven. Whatever your belief is, just enjoy this book for the fiction it is. I hope to return as a more fully developed light force that assists others with their walks. I want to be the spirit that roams the earth to assist others. I want to give back what has been so lovingly provided to me.

It has been six months since my heavenly adventure. I write these last words with a growing satisfaction that the mission God asked of me has been completed as I lay down my pen for the last time. He trusted me to deliver the message, and I do so with honor. He has guided me with every word. I hope, for all who read this book, that you relate it to your life in some way. Our struggles are many. For some, support doesn't seem to be near. I profess to the top of my lungs that your higher power is within you. Whatever religion, faith, or belief that sustains you, use this book's message to strengthen you in that belief. We all struggle with the unseen. But if you have, as the bible says, the faith of a mustard seed, you can remove mountains. It is the conviction of your belief that must decide your destination. Some believe heaven is here and now, on earth. Others believe in reincarnation, that you return later as a future relative or other form. There have been many studies of people who have experienced past lives. I think the important fact here is that you believe. Believe in your God, whatever or whoever that is. My belief is in the trinity, yours may be in Buddhism. I judge not any of those, for I have found God has many ways of showing himself to us. He is different with each person. You reflect in him, so we see and know him only to ourselves. My relationship with him may not hold the same meaning as yours does. All I know is that there is a higher power guiding us and delivering us exactly where we need to go.

Hold these words that I write as a promise that you are loved. You are loved far more than you can imagine. Each individual has their own special place in time and life. May your journey fill the destiny you are meant to live.

With this, Lydia laid down her pen and died, going home to Christi and Brad.

THE END

OR

THE BEGINNING

About The Author

Linda Mayo

I grew up in the small town of Waynesboro, Virginia. I have one daughter whose name was used in the book, and is the joy of my life. While having a successful career in finance, I have always had the desire to write. Out of that desire, I began taking novel writing courses, which pushed me to begin this book. The words flowed to the paper with ease. Was it divinely given? I don't know, but the words came out of no preplan for writing it. Each day my lunch hour created this interesting work of fiction/religious theology and created a path that I hope enters many of your hearts.